BEYOND

THE TIPPING POINT

Doug Hellie

1

Federal Judge Franklin Biermann, feared potentate of the Western Judicial District of Texas, awakened with a start, lifting his head from the table dominating the small, windowless space. His bladder was bursting as he stood abruptly and pondered his whereabouts. It was the safe room in the bowels of the Austin federal court complex, but how long had he been locked in here? Surely for hours and hours.

He hastened to the small bathroom to find the door locked. "Hurry up in there!" he barked to the court clerk, his sole companion in this lockdown situation. There was no response. He rattled the door handle and shouted.

Listening carefully, he could hear deep snoring from inside and shouted some more, banging loudly on the locked door. No amount of noise disturbed the rhythm of the snoring and Biermann remembered the clerk had imbibed heavily of the liquor in the safe room's small refrigerator. The fool had evidently locked himself in and passed out.

Biermann looked around desperately for someplace to urinate. Other than a tiny plastic waste basket, nothing suggested itself. He pounded on the bathroom door some more before giving in to the degrading act of pissing into the trash container like some back alley wino. The hot, unventilated room stank as he zipped up. How dare they treat a federal judge like this?

He would make someone pay dearly for this indignity and this brainless incarceration. The door to the hallway was still locked from outside and the phone to the outside still dead. No one had checked on them since that boob of a marshal had ushered them in and taken away their cell phones. That man would be looking for a new career, Biermann vowed. The same with the drunken clerk in the bathroom. Biermann would institute one hell of an investigation of the entire fiasco, from top to bottom.

Biermann realized he was starving. Though a tough minded man, Biermann was past seventy and unaccustomed to physical discomfort. He yanked the door of the refrigerator open and studied the contents just to make sure he hadn't overlooked anything. No food, candy, or juice, just several hundred miniature bottles of booze. The clerk had accounted for perhaps thirty bottles, the empties now floating in Biermann's piss in the waste basket, but there was still a huge supply.

It was as if someone who knew of Biermann's drinking problem had arranged this situation deliberately. Adding insult was that the fridge was loaded with bottom shelf stuff, not decent for drinking straight and likely to ruin whatever it was mixed with...Rebel Yell, Ancient Age, Early Times, and the like. He'd earlier toyed with a bottle but hadn't indulged, knowing what it could lead to. He hadn't been famished then, or thirsty, making it easier to resist. Now, his body cried out for him to put something into his stomach. The only other drink was water from the tap in the bathroom, currently beyond reach unless he could break the door in.

He licked his dry lips, the trove of booze calling to him. He finally gave in and grabbed a bottle of Ten High, twisting off the tiny cap and sucking it dry in one go. As he pitched the empty aside and snatched a fresh bottle, feeling giddy and out of control, he knew this was not going to end well.

****

Eight blocks from the trapped Biermann, Rajiv Patel snuck up on his friend with a latte in either fist. "Good morning, Bob!" he announced, thrusting one of the hot cups at the surprised man.

"Lifesaver!" exclaimed the recipient with a grin. "I've been stuck here for nearly two hours already. Look at this line!"

"How could anyone miss it?" Patel laughed, gesturing at the throng stretching for many blocks. "Waiting to get their Anjou Pair, no doubt."

Bob's grin turned to a frown. "Don't even joke about that, Rajiv. You'll start a riot."

A dozen people within earshot turned frowning faces their way.

"Ok, ok, my bad taste," Patel apologized, hands held high in apology as he nearly dropped his coffee.

"This may look like a bunch of tech groupies waiting for the latest device from Apple or Anjou, but this crowd's all about getting their hands on Lone Stars," said Bob, "and the Lone Star is about freedom, while the Anjou Pair is about tyranny."

"You're really sold on this Lone Star thing, Bob, and I'm so curious to know why that I'm playing hooky from the office this morning. And for what it's worth, the Anjou Pair devices contain some pretty slick technology. You should give them another look before you upgrade your smart phone."

"That's the problem with you low information fad chasers, Rajiv. You're mesmerized by a few new tech features while the device containing them tracks and reports on you to the feds, one step closer to mandatory tracking implants," Bob huffed.

"Pretty much the law now, isn't it?"

"Not in Texas. Didn't you see what Governor Longstreet did to his Anjou Pair on TV the other night?"

"That guy's cruisin' for a bruisin'. First, he publicly defies the Shared Responsibility Act by stomping on his tracker and calling for everyone else to join him. Then, over lawsuits and threats from the Justice Department, the Federal Reserve, the SEC, the FDIC, and the rest of the universe, he launches this…" Rajiv trailed off, waving at the massive line of people. "What's the magic about this Lone Star thing, anyway? I thought I'd find you down here with a few dozen people, not thousands."

"Maybe they don't look at things the same way in India, Rajiv," Bob answered, "but in Texas we know that property rights and freedom go hand in hand. You can't have one without the other, and there's no property more personal than your money. Texans are afraid of the dollar. The feds just keep running the printing presses faster and faster because it's the only way to cover their spending, pouring out dollars backed by nothing but empty promises. Lone Stars can't be whipped up out of thin air like dollars. They have a fixed relationship to the gold sitting in the Texas Depository. If the politicians in Texas want to create more Lone Stars, they have to acquire more gold. Honest money. Hard money. Money that maintains its purchasing power. That's the attraction."

"So…," Patel waved his coffee cup at the bank building they were slowly advancing toward, "you are walking out of there with gold coins in your pocket?"

"That would be absurd, wouldn't it?" responded Bob. "Actual gold is far too valuable to be a practical form of currency now that it's at $5,000 an ounce. The beauty of the Lone Star is that it's backed by gold but issued in denominations of useful amounts, roughly one Lone Star to one U.S. dollar at today's exchange rate."

"And you can't go to the Depository and exchange 5,000 Lone Stars for an ounce of gold?" retorted Patel. "How do you even know for sure that the gold is there, and that Texas didn't just print up some pretty paper with a fancy story behind it?"

"There are audit firms making unannounced visits to the Depository all the time, with the results published directly to the Internet. That's a fundamental part of the deal. When is that last time the Federal Reserve was publicly audited, or the U.S. Treasury?"

Patel was lost in thought as they shuffled forward, fewer than fifty people between them and the bank entrance. "Granting all that, what's the attraction for you, Bob? How can you get a practical benefit from this experimental currency? Don't you think it could be volatile and risky, like Bitcoin and the other virtual currencies? A lot of people have lost their shirts holding Bitcoin."

"The Lone Star is a hard currency, Rajiv, not a virtual one. Five thousand Lone Stars to the ounce of gold, fixed in perpetuity. It's the new currency of Texas, the tenth largest economy in the world and one of the fastest growing ones. Not only am I comfortable holding it, I think I can use it to definite financial advantage. When I get in there..." Bob waved at the bank building rising above them, "I plan on exchanging the dollars in my savings account for Lone Stars, and opening a new Lone Star credit line. I'll sit on that awhile and watch my dollar-denominated loan balances drop in value relative to it, which I'm sure is going to happen sooner than later. Maybe in a year I can pay off each dollar of my debt with half of a Lone Star."

Patel snorted, "That would involve a dollar crash, losing 50% against the Lone Star in a year. You're dreaming, Bob!"

"Am I? You would trust unsecured dollars issued by a bankrupt, out-of-control government over gold-backed money sponsored by a solvent, disciplined nation-state? Please!"

"So, you are bailing out entirely on the dollar, Bob? Going whole hog into Lone Stars today?"

"Pay closer attention to what I'm saying, Rajiv. I'm moving my assets – my savings and my cash on hand – into Lone Stars. I'm leaving my mortgage, car loan, and credit cards in dollars because I believe in the near future I'll be able to pay those off with a lot fewer Lone Stars than it would take today."

Patel finished his coffee, frowning in concentration. He finally mumbled, "Maybe I'll tag along into the bank with you and get a few of these Lone Stars for myself."

****

I.M. Schiff, A.G., an arms supplier out of Dusseldorf, Germany, had a contract to supply the state of Texas with upgrades for antiaircraft missile batteries deployed by the Texas State Guard. Payment to Schiff was to be made in Lone Stars to the tune of 50 million LS, a currency Schiff feared might lose value versus dollars or euros. Since Schiff would own Lone Stars at the conclusion of the contract, a rise in their value would be advantageous, but a drop would hurt Schiff's profits. In order to lock in its intended profit on the transaction, Schiff would need to hedge its future receipt of Lone Stars by selling, or "going short", Lone Star futures contracts. If the Lone Star went up against dollars and euros, Schiff would lose money on the short position but make it up on the actual Lone Stars themselves as they gained value. If Lone Stars fell in value against dollars and euros, the gain in the short position would make up for Schiff's loss on the actual Lone Stars. The net effect either way would be Schiff's assurance of making the profit on the contract it had originally calculated before signing the deal with Texas.

The problem was that the U.S. government had forbidden brokers and futures exchanges in the United States from offering Lone Star futures or options, and had prohibited banks with federal charters from financing such activity.

The Texans had worked out an end run around these attempted roadblocks, however.

In the case of the Schiff hedging transaction, the pieces falling into place began with First Longhorn Bank in Austin, a state chartered institution not subject to federal control, extending a ten billion LS line of credit to Deutsche Bank in Frankfurt. As a Deutsche Bank client, Schiff was able to borrow the LS needed to place a 5% down payment, the margin requirement of Schiff's futures broker, on the 50 million Lone Stars worth of futures contracts it was selling short. If Lone Stars moved up in value over time, creating an increasing loss in Schiff's short position, Schiff would borrow more Lone Stars from Deutsche Bank and put them up with Schiff's broker to "maintain", or carry, its futures position. If Lone Stars fell, Schiff's hedge would gain value and no further margin would be required. When Schiff finally received the 50 million LS payment on its Texas contract in a few months, it would buy back its LS futures position for a gain or loss offset precisely by its gain or loss on the physical Lone Stars it received.

When Schiff had sold its 50 million in LS futures contracts on the Eurex Exchange this morning, they had been purchased by a hedge fund out of New York through the hedge fund's broker in London, beyond Washington's reach. The hedge fund manager was convinced Lone Stars would gain fast in value against the dollar and was willing to speculate on that belief. The hedge fund's margin deposit with its broker came from Lone Stars borrowed from Barclays Bank, which itself had borrowed 15 billion LS from First Longhorn in Austin.

The math was compelling for First Longhorn. It had made combined loans to Deutsche Bank and Barclays totaling 25 billion Lone Stars. Against this First Longhorn held a 10% reserve of 2.5 billion physical Lone Stars in its vault, a large chunk of the 30 billion in physical Lone Star "base currency" being issued on this launch day. Other banks in the Lone Star launch syndicate, banks with Texas charters, were doing likewise, spreading access to the new currency around the globe. First Longhorn and the others were earning fees and interest in very healthy amounts on these arrangements while establishing a wide bridgehead for Lone Stars in world finance. When the deal with Kowloon Holdings closed in November and the gold involved became available to back issuance of another 500 billion in Lone Stars, the currency would quickly become a major player in international financial activity, backing trillions in loans and serving as collateral for tens of trillions in futures, options, and swaps put together by hedgers like Schiff and speculators like the New York hedge fund.

Everyone was happy with the arrangement except the U.S. government, which preferred that everyone be forced to deal in dollars over which it had a monopoly. That its abuse of that monopoly had led to creation of the Lone Star in the first place, the government didn't care. It simply became enraged at the notion of competition undercutting its control. Other nations in Europe and Asia guilty of running the printing presses on euros, yen, and other unsecured currencies also viewed the Lone Star with unease. No so much, though, as to prevent profitable Lone Star financing and trading by their banks and exchanges. As to that, they were only too happy to poke the overbearing and untrustworthy U.S. government in the eye and let the new currency rip.

The one man who could have stopped these Lone Star transactions before they started by issuing a federal injunction lay sprawled in a drunken stupor on the floor of a safe house in Austin, surrounded by a pile of dead soldiers as empty as a politician's promise.

2

Situated on 280,000 acres of pine forest straddling the Canoochee River in southeastern Georgia, Fort Stewart served as home to the 3rd Infantry Division of the United States Army. "The Third", which had once bristled with 30,000 soldiers, now comprised only the 3,500 men and women of the 4th Infantry Brigade Combat Team and another two thousand souls pushing paper. The once-mighty division now existed mainly on paper. Over the past decade, the Third's three armored brigades had been demobilized in response to relentless budget cuts in Washington. The entire U.S. Army now possessed only 24 brigade combat teams, down from 45 just 10 years earlier. These 24 combat brigades were evenly divided between armored, mechanized, and light infantry units, the 4th Infantry Brigade being of the latter variety.

4th Brigade was a hybrid between regular army troops and part-time reserves, a further compromise in the struggle against plummeting defense funding. Within the Brigade itself, areas of responsibility were divided between active duty personnel in the logistical, recon, and engineering units, with part-time, "weekend warriors" manning artillery and motorized infantry roles. With President Palma's call up for deployment to Oman, the weekend warriors had been brought to active status and were reporting in from training centers and armories hundreds of miles around. Jobs and civilian lives had been put on hold for an undetermined duration, with all-but-defunct military careers brought back to life by the call up. The 3,000 reservists undertaking full-time duties with 4th Brigade, along with another 97,000 Army reserves, 100,000 active duty soldiers, and 20,000 Marines, brought the expeditionary force to Oman well above the 200,000 minimum promised by the Administration to the Sultanate and its Gulf neighbors. This force would represent fully 80% of the shrunken U.S. military's land offensive capability, leaving scant combat contingents in the Pacific, Europe, and at home.

The administrative area of Fort Stewart resembled a busy college campus on the opening day of the fall term, except that everyone bustling between buildings was in uniform. Lieutenant Colonel Grace Peters, acting commandant of the 4th BCT, watched the activity below from a third floor office window before turning back to the wearying task at hand, the hurried selection of officers and noncoms to take charge of the 4th's battalions, companies, and platoons. When her boss, Brigadier General Forrest Bledsoe, showed up with his staff in a few weeks to take overall command, Peters would drop down and assume command of the Second Battalion. Until then, and with precious little time to get things ready for deployment, she was charged with putting the proper pieces into the right places. That meant mainly getting the right people into position, a task made nearly impossible by the Army's current predicament.

Three presidential administrations in a row, over twenty years, had treated the military with open disdain and hostility, starving it of funds and chopping away wholesale at its personnel and assets. While it was shrinking, the military was becoming increasingly politicized and used for social experimentation. Career officers and noncoms, especially those with combat training or experience, were purged in favor of candidates put forward by the activist elements running Washington.

A new cabinet-level entity brought into existence by radicals in Congress and the White House, the Department of Fairness and Affirmation in Gender Outcomes, had hired and embedded 5,000 investigators throughout the military looking for LGBT-hostile practices, traditions, and terminology. An officer or enlisted person becoming the subject of an "F&A", meaning a "Fairness & Affirmation" investigation or administrative proceeding, suddenly found themselves at a career dead end or forcibly expelled from service. Bringing charges didn't require the production substantive proof, just claims that reached the required level of seriousness, with a low threshold of evidence being enough to result in an affirmative finding. Many of the military's best people didn't wait to be snared, resigning instead in disgust. Distrust was high among those who remained, and morale was abysmal throughout the force.

Colonel Peters had scant bench depth to work with in filling unit commands. She had a bad feeling about the upcoming deployment to the Middle East, as well as the high expectations of her boss to meet, and needed leaders in place able to bring the 4th to fighting capability in a 60 day time frame, itself absurdly insufficient. A decade earlier she could have managed such placements off the top of her head, but nearly all of those people were gone and the ones left unavailable. An exception was Major Ellen Kopechne, Peters' right hand and the acting CO of 2nd Battalion, an all-female frontline combat force.

The "Amazon Battalion", launched with fanfare by the previous president, had been neglected once the favorable PR had abated. Originally comprised 100% of regular, full time troops, it had degenerated into a largely reservist outfit. It hadn't functioned as a fully operating entity in five years and it had never been deployed to a combat zone. Unit commanders had come and gone quickly and the battalion developed a reputation as a place bad for career advancement.

Now that it was assembling full strength and about to debark to a zone of likely hostilities, the nonsense had to stop and everyone aboard needed to shape up fast. Kopechne was the person for the job, fanatical to bring the battalion up to full standards and unafraid of the potential career consequences. Like Peters herself, Kopechne had been the subject of numerous F&A actions from which Peters had bailed her out, just as General Bledsoe had repeatedly done for Peters. Among the dwindling cadre of fighting officers left in the Army, a tacit, mutual protection ethic had developed, headed by flag level officers willing to take the heat to maintain a core level of combat readiness within the force.

The most common charges leveled by the F&A investigators were that certain commanders exercised "toxic leadership" that was too demanding, or promoted environments and practices that were LGBT-hostile. Simply enforcing the Army's physical fitness standards was enough to trigger such complaints, and the result had been the creation of abridged standards for certain categories of troops. Colonel Peters, Major Kopechne, and other line officers had learned the hard way to thread the needle in such circumstances. For the upcoming deployment, General Bledsoe required a change in that policy for which he was ready to take the heat. Those unable to meet combat readiness physically or mentally would not be going along to Oman, at least as part of the 4th Combat Brigade. Nor would there be time to replace them, so leadership of every unit in the brigade from battalions to squads was of critical importance. Achieving compliance with standards while avoiding attrition was the mantra.

Peters and Kopechne had filled most of the slots over the past week, working without much sleep as they reviewed files and checked backgrounds and performance through what was left of the grapevine, flying candidates in to Fort Stewart for interviews and final decisions. They'd started with the other battalions, leaving Second Battalion for last, not wanting to risk accusations of favoring it since Peters would wind up taking charge of it. Their pool of candidates was down to the bottom of the barrel as they dealt with the Second's five companies, each with three platoons. They were finally on the home stretch with Echo Company, where a somewhat politically minded captain, Mahalia Dodge, had been offered command and accepted, and the existing COs of 1st and 2nd Platoons, both second lieutenants, were confirmed as suitable to remain in those posts. Only the troublesome 3rd Platoon lacked a commanding officer, having run through three in the past year. Continuity had only been maintained by the noncom in charge, an overqualified sergeant first class biding her last year of service before reaching her "twenty" and retirement with a full pension. In the matter of commissioned officers, 3rd Platoon had been snake bit for a long time.

By the time Peters and Kopechne got to the matter of the 3rd's commanding officer, they were out of time and out gas, hurrying through the remaining personnel files with the last of their energy. Kopechne finally returned to a particular file and tossed it across the table to Peters.

"How about this one?"

Peters studied it again, this time much more carefully. She had been thinking the same thing, that this one had potential to succeed but also to fail given the driven nature of the candidate in combination with a lack of orthodoxy in carrying out orders. You never knew about someone like this so early in their career, an unorthodox type who could be a dud or a budding Patton. Still, of what was left to choose from, this one clearly didn't lack for initiative.

"Amy McIvor, first lieutenant, in her third year of service," Peters intoned, reading snatches of the dossier aloud to fend off drowsiness. "From an old Tennessee family. Father a graduate of West Point, killed in Afghanistan in 2007, awarded the Silver Star posthumously for saving a squad cut off in an ambush. Mother remarried, practiced law, entered state politics, and…" Peters' voice trailed off in surprise, "…and is leading in the race to be Tennessee's next governor. We've got a pedigreed blue blood here, Ellen. Might be a prima donna," she concluded with doubt in her voice.

"Read further," Kopechne replied.

Peters continued her study silently for a few minutes before smiling and giving a small whistle of appreciation. "She's been better to the Army than the Army's been to her, that's for certain. Shut out of a chance to attend West Point in her father's footsteps because of the changes in the nature of Congressional appointments and the new quotas. Not being a minority or an LGBT put the Point out of reach, so she settled for ROTC at the University of Tennessee and OCS at the University of Alabama. Looks like she took every advanced course in combat doctrine, strategy, tactics, and leadership that she could, earning promotion to first lieutenant in two years on the strength of those efforts. Staff assignments mostly, though she's applied several times for a line command. Fighting hard not be a victim of the Army's endless cuts in personnel, especially in the junior officer corps."

Peters paused to refill her cup with burnt coffee from the drip machine on the sideboard before returning to the McIvor file with a chuckle. "This last part cracks me up, though I'm sure Lieutenant McIvor wasn't laughing given the likely consequences. In charge of a six vehicle convoy moving high priority cargo from Fort Knox to Fort Campbell."

"Yeah," Kopechne chimed in. "Crates full of gold."

"We don't know that, though I wouldn't bet against it. Anyway, shipping cargo heavy enough to cause a lot breakdowns in those old trucks," Peters summarized aloud as she scanned the file. "McIvor had two Humvees for escorts and four duece-and-a-halfs, fully loaded. One breaks down so she has another truck tow it, which causes it to break down, too. There's no help coming for hours and the delivery's going to be late, so our girl takes the initiative and flags down a passing eighteen wheeler hauling an empty flatbed trailer in the direction of Fort Campbell. Offers the diesel in the tanks of the two dead trucks in return for the guy hauling them to Campbell under escort by the remaining vehicles. She gets the cargo to Campbell on time and promptly catches hell for misappropriation of 400 gallons of Army fuel, even though she didn't tie up any of the Army's tow trucks as she could have. Now she's got to be worried sick she might have put the nail in the coffin of her budding career."

"She's back at Fort Knox, still assigned to the motor pool," said Kopechne. "We couldn't get her down here until tomorrow at earliest for an interview."

"Do you think we need an interview first? Is there another candidate running a close second?"

"Not really. I'm willing to gamble on her gratitude and ability if we bail her out of her current predicament. I'll call her right now and make the offer if you concur."

Peters sipped her bitter brew, tossing the file back across the table and sinking lower in her chair in exhaustion, relieved to be finished with the marathon effort. "Let's do it."

****

Bin Lao, Acting President of the Peoples Republic of China, reread a copy of Judge Biermann's order for the immediate sale of 30,000 acres of the Triple M Ranch in Texas to Kowloon Holdings in Hong Kong for a paltry two million dollars, including all mineral rights. Under those acres sat at least a hundred billion dollars' worth of rare earth elements which would further China's global monopoly and make the shareholders of Kowloon even more wealthy than they already were, and even more beholden to the Bin-Wang political faction, which pulled Kowloon's strings.

Bin gazed with great satisfaction at his surroundings in the sumptuous, cavernous presidential office, brightly lit against the smoggy darkness of daytime Beijing outside of the floor-to-ceiling windows. President Chen was in a medically induced coma from which he might never emerge, victim of a heinous attack on the ancient streets of Qufu by the Taiping terrorist group. The event had been kept secret, the excuse for Chen's sudden absence given vaguely as "a short leave for minor medical treatment and vacation." While Chen lay in a coma, his powerful ally, Shin Kuo, Premier of the State Council, rallied opposition to Bin and had so far prevented an outright takeover of the government by Bin and his own close ally, General Wang Dong, Vice Chairman of the Central Military Commission and China's highest ranking military officer. A rise in the value of Kowloon shares couldn't come soon enough. Shin was a dangerous impediment to Bin's plans.

While he occupied this office he would do everything possible to consolidate his position and advance his aggressive agenda. First and foremost was to get the Clingman Mine project in Texas off to a very fast start. Second was to move China's gold reserves secretly from the vaults of the Peoples Bank of China, located in Beijing and Shanghai, to Kowloon's high security vault on the island of New Beijing half a world away. Should Shin somehow prevail over the Bin-Wang faction politically, he would find that Bin Lao held an economic hole card with the nation's gold reserves under lock and key in a distant location. Combined with the gold recently extracted from the Americans as bond collateral, the entire contents of Fort Knox and the Federal Reserve, minus a chunk diverted to Texas, there would be 20,000 tons in Kowloon's custody. The shipment would travel deep in the holds of the many warships comprising the Peoples Liberation Army Navy, the PLAN, as they assembled and traveled en masse to the Caribbean Sea for a global show of force concurrent with New Beijing's grand opening. The artificial island would sport not only the world's most sophisticated commercial port, trading venue, and banking center, but highly advanced military facilities as well, aimed directly at America's soft underbelly.

General Wang was ushered in and Bin rose to greet his colleague, handing him the copy of the Biermann's judicial order.

"We are on our way, General. It is all coming together very quickly," chortled Bin. "A ship loaded with construction equipment and engineers has just left New Beijing for Corpus Christi. The Pentagon has been ordered by President Palma to establish a no fly zone over Clingman and an exclusive air corridor from the Texas coast overland to the mining complex. Commercial air traffic will be required to stay above 30,000 feet. The State Department in Washington will soon declare Clingman a Chinese Exclusive Economic Autonomous Zone with full diplomatic status. What of the fleet?"

"Admiral Huang assures me he will weigh anchor and depart on schedule in five weeks," Wang replied. "He will conduct training maneuvers enroute while crossing the Pacific, then transit the fleet through the Nicaragua Canal, giving that project its first major piece of traffic. Our gold reserves will be offloaded and safe in Kowloon's vaults within a week of the fleet's arrival. None but Admiral Huang know of its true nature. Like the Americans did with their gold when they stripped it from Fort Knox, we have crated ours marked as heavy weapons and ordinance."

Tea was brought and the two sat in satisfied silence, sipping from small cups and gazing into the brilliant future.

3

The lockdown of the federal courthouse and adjacent blocks in downtown Austin finally ended early on Saturday morning, after no additional explosive devices had been found for 24 hours. Special Agent Harwood of the FBI wasted no time finding Major Briscoe of the Texas State Guard, who'd been in charge of the emergency response that prevented Harwood from following President Palma's order to extract Judge Biermann from the courthouse safe room on Thursday night. Harwood hadn't been able to make phone contact with the judge in the last two days, either, assuming Briscoe had handled those communications.

When he finally had Briscoe's attention, Harwood decided it was best to adopt a jocular tone. "I'll bet Judge Biermann's been chewing your ear off."

Briscoe was stone-faced. "I haven't spoken with him."

"Well," responded Harwood, taken aback, "whoever has been checking in on him surely relayed the judge's displeasure to you."

"No one's been checking on him."

"Good God, man, why the hell not?"

"Agent Harwood, the judge was safe in the safe room and we had our hands full looking for explosive devices in a ten block area. You're welcome to go and let him know it's safe to come out."

Harwood, tailed by two of his men, did just that. Finding the safe room involved a couple of false turns even with the schematic he'd been given. He would have had a U.S. marshal lead them but none were present as yet. Locating the door, he knocked and waited for a response that didn't come. There was an emergency phone mounted down the hallway and he punched in the safe room number only to get a dial tone. Finally, he called the senior marshal on his cell phone, who was at home mowing his lawn and seemed surprised the courthouse had been reopened.

"Is Judge Biermann okay?" he asked Harwood, who bit back an angry reply.

"Look, I'm not getting anyone to open the door or answer the safe room phone. I need you and your team down here and I need the entry code for this door."

After a delay while the senior marshal went to find the number, with a barking dog and shouting children in the background, Harwood was given the access number. He punched it in, opened the safe room door, and was hit by a stench so vile he nearly vomited.

On the floor lay Franklin Biermann surrounded by a hundred or more tiny bottles, all empty. There were puddles of drying vomit and a small waste basket that appeared to have been used as a urinal until it overflowed, soaking the carpet beneath. The air conditioning was off and the humid air reeked of ammonia and vomit.

"Jesus!" cried one the agents behind Harwood before bending over and puking against the wall.

"Watch out!" cried the other agent as a small door, apparently to a bathroom, suddenly swung open and a disheveled, mousy looking man stepped out.

"Oh, thank God! Have you got any food?" the man implored.

"Food? What…" Harwood was too flummoxed to respond, the mention of food tugging at his gag reflex. "Who the hell are you, and what happened in here?"

"He went berserk after he started drinking," the man replied, pointing to the unconscious figure on the floor. "I had to stay locked in there or he would have assaulted me. He nearly broke the door down several times. We were stuck in this safe room with no way to open the door or call outside, and nothing in the refrigerator but booze."

"Check Biermann's vitals," Harwood barked at the agent who was recovering from losing his breakfast against the wall. He turned back to the refugee from the bathroom and gestured to the bottles scattered on the floor. "Are you telling me the Judge Biermann drank all of these, without any food or water in the past two days?"

"I had a few at first, but not after he trapped me in the bathroom. It's obvious what happened, isn't it? Look at him. He turned into some kind of animal after the first few bottles. It was hell."

"He's breathing unevenly," said the agent crouched over Biermann, knees wet from the carpet and determined to burn his suit when he got out of here. "Pulse is thready."

"Call EMS. Tell them we've got a V.I.P., age around 70, with acute alcohol poisoning and dehydration," ordered Harwood, stalking away from the room and its vile smell. The head of the U.S. Marshal contingent had a lot of explaining to do, and blame to accept.

The bathroom refugee tried to follow but the other agent stopped him. "Stay put. We've got a lot of questions for you."

"I've got to have something to eat. I'm not feeling right."

He began to shake violently before staggering into the hallway and collapsing.

"For God's sake," rasped the agent before bellowing down the hall for medical assistance. The other agent was throwing up on the wall again.

****

President Jay Palma was as furious as Vance Carling had ever seen him, left cheek twitching madly as Carling delivered the news from Austin.

"Are you telling me the son of a bitch was DRUNK?"

"That's what the FBI is reporting, Jay. Biermann was locked in the safe room for two days with no way to get out. The phone was somehow not connected and there was no food or water, just a couple hundred of those little liquor bottles like the airlines sell on long flights."

"How convenient. And all Biermann could do about the situation was drink himself into a coma? I hope he dies!"

"Well, he might."

"Surely now we can get some other judge down there to issue an injunction stopping these damned Lone Stars, Vance."

Carling hesitated to answer. It was bad form to bring Palma nothing but bad news. The messenger ran the distinct risk of getting shot. Figuratively speaking, of course, though Carling had no wish to test that assumption given Palma's demeanor.

"Checking with our contacts down there, Jay, it doesn't sound like there's another federal judge in the district who will touch it unless Biermann agrees to it. Everyone's terrified of crossing him."

Palma hunched over his desk, eyes hooded and left cheek flickering like a violent thunderstorm.

Carling pressed on. "Anyway, where the Lone Star's concerned, the cat's out of the bag anyway. They issued 30 billion of the things Friday either in currency or as loan collateral to banks."

"Our banks are prohibited from doing Lone Star transactions or even so much as holding the fucking things," Palma snarled, ending with a hissing click like an enraged snapping turtle.

"True, but banks with state charters got involved in a big way, and so did a bunch of big banks in Europe and Asia. Lone Star futures and options are going strong in Hong Kong, Shanghai, London, and in the Eurex market. There are a lot of big players who've jumped in already, Jay. Unwinding all of that could lead to real grief."

"Damn Biermann anyway!" Palma snapped, slapping his hand loudly on the desk. "This can't be allowed to stand. Tell those doctors down there to get that asshole back on his feet and into the courtroom. If we move quick, we can still cap this off and undo the damage."

Carling was taken aback. "Jay, Biermann's an old man and very sick...we don't want a replay of what happened with Al Morse."

Carling instantly regretted saying that. He should've cut out his tongue first. Mention of Al Morse was like a red flag to a bull.

Palma fixed him with gorgon eyes. "Do as you're told, and get the hell out of my office."

****

Monday evening while taking a break from the campaign and cogitating over coffee in his K Street office in downtown DC, Paul Jovian received an unusual call. As manager of Palma's reelection campaign and the most highly paid political consultant in America, Jovian didn't any longer seek connections so much as they sought him. The voice on the other end of this call represented the very apex of government-connected capitalism in America and perhaps the world, speaking with an aristocratic Boston accent much like a Kennedy. Jovian didn't know the caller's name, privately labeling him "Blue Blood", and had only spoken with him a few times. Blue Blood always initiated the call, and had never given Jovian a return number. Blue Blood represented the economic uber elite Jovian and his close circle simply referred to as "The Interests."

"Good evening, Mr. Jovian," said Blue Blood.

"Good evening, sir."

"How is the campaign going?"

"Very well. No major problems."

"No? How is Al Morse doing? We've been unable to get in touch with him."

Jovian had long surmised that Morse was the main contact between the DC establishment and The Interests. "I've been out of touch with Al myself, sir, but it happens from time to time. He operates that way on occasion. Always has."

"We certainly hope that's the case, and that he'll be available next time we call him."

"I'll pass that along. Shall I mention it to the president?"

"No, but you can mention to President Palma that it's time to leave the Lone Star currency alone."

Jovian was too shocked to speak. Morse had always intimated that The Interests were dead set against the Lone Star and had been since it was just an idea being tossed around by the Texans. Morse claimed that they'd been cranking up the pressure on the Palma Administration to stop it as it gained momentum.

"Leave it alone?" he asked, seeking clarification in case he'd misunderstood.

"Let it take hold as it will, and let U.S. banks and exchanges in on the action," Blue Blood said. "That is the policy we strongly prefer going forward. Please make sure President Palma understands our strong feelings on the matter."

Jovian swallowed hard as he visualized conveying this message to Palma, who'd invested so much of his credibility and political capital in stopping the Lone Star, sadly without effect. Maybe he'd hand the job of informing Palma of this sea change off to Vance Carling, who seemed better able to navigate Palma's eruptions and come out alive.

"I will make sure the president hears of it, sir."

The line went dead. Jovian set the phone down and leaned back in his chair, mind racing. What it must mean, he decided, was what one of his competitors, a consultant who had also received calls from Blue Blood, had once theorized over cocktails. The Interests had diversified their constituency to include the rising Asian, Latin American, and Middle Eastern interests alongside the original American and European ones. These new interests didn't always see eye to eye with the old ones. Preserving the hegemony of the dollar in global finance had suddenly lost priority, either because money making opportunities abounded with the advent of the Lone Star on world markets, or because the consensus had evolved that the dollar was dying, or some combination of both. The abrupt about face also indicated rifts among the Interests.

Jovian felt a thrill of horror at the implications, and decided to give the Texas currency a hard look. Despite having more than a billion dollars in the bank, he suddenly felt less secure than he had for a long time.

4

Entering the building that housed 2nd Battalion's administrative offices, Sergeant 1st Class Eleanda "Elly" Gonzales was not hard for Lieutenant McIvor to spot. The sergeant was a tall, well-built woman of 37 with short hair and a handsome face. From the way she moved, she was clearly in top shape and all business. McIvor had read her file. Born in Ciudad Juarez to an ailing mother, father unknown, and smuggled across the river to be raised by an aunt in El Paso. She enlisted in the Army at 18, gaining combat experience in Afghanistan and the Philippines. She'd received training alongside Special Forces units in battlefield tactics, hand-to-hand fighting, and small unit leadership. Her stellar record should have taken her to the level of master sergeant save for a lack of the political aptitude necessary in an over-politicized army. Submerging those under her control to extensive physical and weapons training, while sparing them hours of diversity and inclusiveness classes, had kept Gonzales a mere E-7 as she struggled to complete twenty years of active service. She had a failed marriage, not unusual for those in the military with its long deployments, and an 8 year old son being raised by the same aunt in El Paso that had raised her.

McIvor was impressed by the sergeant's resume, but leery about the way her career had dead-ended, wondering if her attitude might have become jaded as a result. Such a thing might rub off on the platoon. Gonzales had been with 3rd Platoon for over a year and running it all but single-handedly as commanding officers came and went. The present condition of the platoon would tell McIvor a lot about the efficacy of Sergeant Gonzales.

Likewise, Gonzales had learned what she could about her new commanding officer, who had risen to first lieutenant barely two years out of OCS, either through merit or likelier through connections. It didn't escape Sergeant Gonzales that McIvor was the daughter of a decorated West Pointer, killed in Afghanistan, and a politically prominent mother likely to be the next governor of Tennessee. To appearances, the blond-haired, blue-eyed woman of 24 had an air of seriousness that Gonzales liked, but only time would tell if she was a prima donna, an earnest dud, or a real officer. Whatever the circumstances of McIvor's situation, Gonzales didn't envy anyone, even with connections, struggling as a junior officer in these times of deep cuts. There weren't enough active duty commands to go around, and even a standout had to take what there was, all too often command of a reserve unit such as 3rd Platoon had essentially become.

The 3rd was a weapons unit, and its part-timers were a physical lot, factory and warehouse workers and girls off of farms and ranches, and even one amateur boxer. They had to be physical in order to handle the heavy mortars and antitank rocket launchers that were their stock in trade. At least they didn't have to march afoot. Like the rest of the Army, they moved in trucks, personnel carriers, and small command vehicles, though classified as infantry.

Gonzales had hoped to end her career in better circumstances, or even to transition out to a career on the civilian side of federal service. Her one attempt at that had been a rude shock. Her spouse, Jorge, had been an adjunct instructor of Spanish Literature at UTEP in El Paso, stuck with babysitting duties during her long and frequent deployments. The tension had finally reached boiling point and Jorge had delivered an ultimatum. Get another job or look for another husband.

She had interviewed for a job with the DEA in El Paso, noting two dozen openings being recruited for. It would actually pay substantially better than military service. On meeting with the DEA bureaucrat in charge of hiring, she was told the position was tentatively filled but thanks for coming. When Gonzales mentioned the other two dozen positions being advertised, she was treated to a shocking bit of candor.

"I'll be up front with you, but only because of your military service," said the bureaucrat. "Just between you and me and off the record, those other positions are legacy positions. The position you applied for was our mandatory token opening, and as I just told you, it's very likely filled."

"Legacy positions?" Gonzales had asked.

"Yeah, you know. Reserved for the children of existing employees."

"That's a federal hiring practice, handing down jobs from one generation to the next?" Gonzales was incredulous.

"That's the way it is these days. Off the record of course. I just don't want to see someone like you getting your hopes up when you see a bunch of federal job postings. We're all unionized now, you know. It all goes hand in hand."

So a disillusioned Gonzales had fled back to the dubious security of the devil she knew, the United States Army, and lost her marriage in the bargain. Now, she limited her ambition to getting a full pension on hitting her twenty and a part-time civilian job in the security field after retirement. Finishing out the last year of her career had just gotten a lot more interesting with the upcoming deployment.

She saluted her new CO, who smiled and shook hands warmly enough, and Gonzales showed her to the bullpen where 3rd Platoon's three admin desks were situated, one for each of them and one occupied by a paper pushing corporal. The Lieutenant was anxious to meet the platoon, but Gonzales recommended they hold off until the evening when everyone had reported in. Instead, she suggested, they should tackle a pile of paperwork on McIvor's desk, a stack filled with orders, reports, and manifests. Fresh coffee in hand, they dug into the pile.

The Chief of Police for the municipality of Clingman, Texas, commanded a force of one, that being himself. Joe Bob Sparks shared a small office on Clingman's main drag and only street with Terry Sanchez, the Brewster County Sheriff's Deputy assigned to the Clingman area. A third desk was occasionally used by whomever the Texas Highway Patrol chose to send down. Today it sat empty.

Excitement in the small community was just settling down after the multiple murders and fire out at the Triple M Ranch west of town. The prominent, if degenerate, owner of the storied ranch, Cooney Moore, had managed to get himself tangled up in some kind of drug ring and along with his wife had paid the price. Sparks found the theory full of holes, but it was a federal case and out of his bailiwick.

For one thing, Moore wasn't sharp enough to be any sort of kingpin or even a deputy of a kingpin. He did own a 104,000 acre ranch passed down through five generations, but that was purely luck of the draw. The guy himself was just a hopeless, hapless drug addict and boozer. So was Tammy Mae, his spouse. Other than falling way behind with their drug supplier, Sparks couldn't see any reason that would get them killed in the way they had been.

Even weirder was the involvement of the feds. They'd blocked the gates to the ranch and posted guards to prevent entry, as if the entire vast acreage of the place was a crime scene. Sparks had heard a rumor that air traffic wasn't allowed in the skies over the region encompassing the ranch, the town of Clingman, or points east. He was on the phone to a contact in the Texas Air Guard, seeing if he knew anything, when the office began to shake and rumbling pierced the walls.

A column of eighteen wheelers with flatbed trailers was coming down the main drag and turning at the junction with the road headed west toward the Triple M Ranch. Aboard them was all manner of excavation and earth moving equipment, loads so heavy the ground shook at their passing. The noise was intense and the column stretched back out of sight. Next in the procession came loaded gravel trucks and water tankers, odd looking military-type vehicles pulling sealed trailers, and buses with blocked windows. Escorting the whole shebang were Humvees and motorcycles apparently driven by U.S. Army military police.

Like the rest of the town, Sparks and Sheriff's Deputy Sanchez watched awestruck as the invasion rolled on and on, several hundred vehicles in all. Local traffic was diverted out of the way by the M.P.s and forced to park wherever they could. Sparks approached one of M.P.s and shouted above the racket.

"What is this all about?"

The M.P. looked him over before answering with a shout of his own. "New owners taking possession, sir!"

"New owners of what?"

Instead of answering, the M.P. keyed his radio and spoke into it. Turning back to Sparks, he shouted "Wait one, sir!"

A few minutes later they were joined by a captain. The officer asked if they could step back into Sparks' office to converse away from the noise. Sparks ushered him in and shut the door, relieved at the reduced decibel level. They introduced themselves.

"First, Captain, I want to register my protest regarding all of this pandemonium. I wasn't informed that this gigantic convoy would be coming though. Second, what the hell is going on? Your man out there said something about new owners coming in."

"I'm sorry you weren't informed, Chief Sparks. You were supposed to have been notified yesterday at the latest. We're tasked with escorting convoys from Corpus Christi across south Texas and onto the Triple M Ranch. Get used to it because we've got several convoys scheduled, more than a hundred of them at last count. You can expect half a dozen of them a day for the foreseeable future. They have diplomatic standing and can't be interfered with. You'll be getting notification from the State Department on that."

"Who are they?"

"They're a Chinese conglomerate named Kowloon Holdings. They're taking possession of the western portion of the ranch, the big mesa out there, which they just acquired."

"I've heard nothing of this, Captain. The last I knew, the ranch was a crime scene. The owner was only killed a little over a week ago. I never heard he was in negotiations with Kowloon or anyone else to sell part of the ranch. In fact, rumor had it he would never sell any of it."

"That's above my pay grade, Chief. My orders are to escort them. The Highway Patrol's been cooperating with us on the run from Corpus to here. Best you talk to them. I've got to get back."

As the captain left several locals pushed past him into the small office.

"What in hell is going on, Sparks?" demanded a red-faced Bill Burris, owner of the town's only gas station and convenience store. "All this traffic is blocking people from getting to my pumps and into the store. It's like the Martians are landing out there! I swear, every one of those trucks is being driven by some oriental guy."

****

Paul Jovian decided he couldn't stomach a direct meeting with Jay Palma on Blue Blood's demand that the president reverse his Lone Star policy, and wound up in Vance Carling's office instead. He had to repeat the gist of his conversation with Blue Blood twice before it sank in.

"You're sure you got it right, what they want?" demanded Carling in a hectoring tone, showing rare anger. "Let the Lone Star go unchallenged and compete with the dollar right here within our national borders? It's unthinkable!"

"I know, but he was crystal clear about it, Vance. There must have been some kind of tug of war in boardrooms around the world and this change in policy is the result. Too much money to be made shorting the dollar and the other paper currencies against a gold-backed one."

"I can barely get my head around that idea. How do you intend to convey this information to Jay? Why were you getting a call of that magnitude anyway? That's too big a thing to funnel through a consultant."

Jovian ignored the slight. "They haven't been able to reach Al Morse, and they've been trying frantically. Any chance we can talk to Al and let him deal with Jay on this?" Jovian pleaded.

"No. Al's taking a breather from things. We can't disturb him with this."

"If that's the case, then I ask you to bring this up with Jay. This sort of thing isn't my department, Vance. I've got my hands full with the campaign."

You chicken shit son of a bitch, Carling thought, trying to keep the disgust out of his face. Stick me with this pile of shit so I can get my head chopped off while you hide out in your campaign war room, collecting your obscene fees.

Still, Jovian was right. This wasn't his department, he did have his hands full, and this time Morse wasn't available to help him and provide guidance. Jovian had to come up with plausible reasons why Palma couldn't show up for a debate, his one debate appearance in the 2024 campaign having turned into a debacle as he went off script and tried to wing it. Speeches had to be kept to a minimum in tightly controlled venues, and live interviews were out of the question. Without Morse to stand in, there would be a vacuum where all major campaign activities were concerned. Palma was too much of a loose cannon and with his growing unpopularity they just couldn't afford the risk. The media smelled blood and only copious bribes were keeping them in line and on board, a huge flow of advertising dollars, charitable contributions, and old fashioned suitcases of cash and offshore wire transfers. It was making a big dent in Jovian's 100 billion dollar war chest, which he was already hinting might be insufficient to guarantee a victory.

"Fine, Paul. I'll confirm this directive and pass it along to Jay for you."

"You're not doing it for *me*, Vance. I'm just the recipient of the message."

"Spin it however you like. You'll owe me big time."

****

Carling found Palma huddled with General Hakito, Chairman of the Joint Chiefs of Staff. Palma waved Carling in to join them.

"I'm just checking with General Hakito on what we know about security at the Texas Depository," Palma chirped, looking flushed and hyper to Carling while Hakito looked less than comfortable. "Biermann's still in the hospital and Lone Star activity just keeps growing, especially overseas. We may need to take a more direct approach to shutting Longstreet's pet project down."

"Uh, we should probably have a one-on-one chat about that, Jay," stuttered Carling.

Palma stared at Carling for a moment before turning back to Hakito. "You were saying something about the Texas Guard deployment at the Depository, general."

"We know they've got a thousand man battalion permanently stationed at the Depository, Mr. President, armed with a variety of weapons from tanks and artillery to machine guns to mortars. It's a very secure facility."

"Could it be attacked from the air?" Palma asked, rocking in his chair like an overexcited child. "You know, an airborne assault to occupy it quickly."

Hakito gave an uneasy smile. "We're just talking hypothetically, of course."

"Yeah, yeah, of course," said Palma with an impatient wave.

"An air assault would be infeasible as well as illegal, if you're expecting the U.S. military to be involved. That said, we've received information in the last week that the Guard has deployed upgraded S-300 batteries all around the Depository grounds, so aerial assault is out of the question."

"S-300s?" Palma rocked back as if he'd been slapped. "What the hell business does Longstreet have with antiaircraft missiles? Where did he get them? From the Russians?"

"Evidently they were purchased from a German arms company that originally got them from the Russians and upgraded them. There are further upgrades being performed from what we know, to keep them state-of-the-art."

"Is it even legal for a state to acquire sophisticated arms like that?" Palma demanded to know, having turned to Carling, who raised his hands with a shrug. He noticed Palma's left cheek beginning to twitch. Palma turned back to Hakito.

"So you're telling me that Longstreet's gold is sown up tight down there, with no feasible way of snatching it?"

"About the size of it, Mr. President. Fort Knox has nothing on the Texas Depository from what I can see. I'm sure there are other, better ways to address your issues with the Lone Star currency," Hakito ventured. "Perhaps you should brainstorm with Vice President Morse on it."

Carling cringed.

Palma's expression turned frosty. "That will be enough, General Hakito. You're dismissed."

The general staged a quick retreat in the face of Palma's sudden hostility, unable to understand how he might have offended the president but certain he had managed to do so.

When they were alone, Palma turned to Carling, left cheek rippling with tension. "What did you want to see me about?" he asked tersely.

Carling gave him a quick and very positive update on campaign developments. The change of policy Blue Blood had demanded regarding the Lone Star could wait until a better time. Carling had never been suicidal.

****

"Is this all of them?" Judge Biermann demanded of the U.S. marshal in charge of security for the federal court complex in

Austin. He lay in a hospital bed for a seventh day, an IV tube still attached as they slowly detoxed and rehydrated him after the safe room ordeal. The marshal was showing him photos of his entire contingent. The man who had flashed his badge at Biermann and the court clerk late on Thursday afternoon, when the first bombs had been found, and who had hustled them into the safe room, was not among those pictured.

"This is all of them, sir. The man who escorted you to the safe room must have been an imposter."

"No shit!" barked Biermann, feeling crappy and unable to abide this fool. "I want a full investigation of how an imposter obtained one of your badges, got into the facility, tampered with the supplies in the safe room refrigerator, doctored the door lock, and cut off the phone. Also, why did no one check in on us for two days? What dumb shit came up with that policy? We nearly died in there! I want names, facts, findings, and your signature at the bottom of that report, and I want it all yesterday, do you read me?"

The marshal packed away the photos with as much dignity as he could muster, nodded to the judge, and left knowing his career had probably just taken a terminal hit.

As the marshal left, a clerk entered with a thick file. Not the clerk who'd locked himself in the safe room bathroom. That cretin had been fired already.

"What is that?" Biermann snapped, not liking the size of the file. He wasn't up to dealing with complex matters yet.

"It's the Lone Star injunction, sir, the one you were working on when…events interrupted you last Thursday. What do you want me to do with it?"

"Use it for toilet paper. Where's that damned nurse with my lunch?"

5

Admiral Hanrahan and General Bartz were in civvies, riding in a golf cart at a very private club west of Gainesville in the Virginia countryside. Both would've preferred the Army Navy Country Club in the heart of Fairfax and next door to the Pentagon, but privacy trumped convenience given the business at hand. Each imagined the other had received the same offer from the oily attaché from the Iraqi Embassy, that unsavory Tikriti fellow. One hundred million dollars to mismanage army logistics in the case of Bartz, and divert navy ships away from the Arabian Sea and the Gulf of Oman in the case of Hanrahan. Neither could foresee any real harm coming from these machinations. Both had grievances to salve with the forthcoming pile of money.

The soaring career of General Bartz had been ended by a drunken, anti-gay slur overheard in a Georgetown bar one night when he groused that "no one can get ahead in the army anymore unless they're a butt fucker or a cunt licker," after which he was besieged by investigators from FAGO, his impolitic term for the Department of Fairness and Affirmation in Gender Outcomes. He was soon informed by the Pentagon hierarchy that his fast track days were over, and was shunted into a high level but dead-end post in charge of logistics for the Oman deployment. Tikriti soon found him and invited him to a round of golf at this very club, making his slimy offer and handing Bartz a shiny debit card as an earnest money down payment.

"It has $100,000 available on it, my good friend," said Tikriti with smarmy grin. "All I ask is that you spend it discreetly and avoid attracting undo attention. And here," Tikriti handed over a smartphone linked to an offshore bank account, "is where you can track deposits being made to your new numbered account as you fulfill your end of the agreement."

The balance already stood at $5 million, though Bartz couldn't access the funds until the completion of the deal. Upon completion, Bartz was promised the code unlocking the account. The sight of the multimillion dollar sum already sitting there gave him a warm feeling and the stirrings of a hard on as he thought of the pleasures he could buy with such a fortune. All he had to do was send Oman-bound troops to an encampment near the capital of Muscat in eastern Oman, and the equipment, munitions, and supplies to a depot north of Thumrait in the western part of the country. Soon enough the troops and their gear would be reunited, no real harm done, and Bartz could retire superrich and thumb his nose at the top brass who'd derailed him on his way to becoming Chairman of the Joint Chiefs of Staff.

Hanrahan's deal had been identical, his task to get the U.S. Navy's carrier strike forces away from Oman and the Arabian Sea. Hanrahan's sin, career-wise, had been to seek favor with the Palma Administration by concocting spurious rationales for sharp reductions in the size of the fleet. The administration had been only too happy to jump aboard, resulting in the early retirement of six *Nimitz* Class supercarriers and their escorting ships from active service while delaying construction of their replacements. The Chief of Naval Operations and his cohorts never forgave Hanrahan, freezing him at the level of Deputy CNO until they could figure a way to force him from active duty. Meanwhile, Hanrahan had played on the desire of President Palma and his special advisor, Vance Carling, to conduct the Oman deployment on the cheap and divert the savings toward facilitating Palma's reelection campaign. The *Obama* Carrier Strike Group would depart the Gulf region earlier than planned and not be replaced by the *Roosevelt* Carrier

Strike Group as originally scheduled. The *Roosevelt* CSG would instead be utilized for several months for a glorified boatlift of refugees from Latin America to the U.S. There would be a gap of 5 to 6 months without an aircraft carrier in the Oman region, but Hanrahan wasn't worried since the Omanis themselves were well equipped to provide necessary cover for U.S. forces, possessing fighter wings of F16s and advanced antiaircraft missile batteries. Anyway, there really wasn't any shit to hit the fan over there, just some camel jockeys playing at jihad over the border in Yemen. Nothing the Army couldn't handle, carrier support or not. Hanrahan had been looking at eight figure real estate listings in the Caribbean islands in anticipation of receiving his payout.

Tikriti had made Bartz and Hanrahan aware of one another and charged them with cooperation in the carrying out of their respective missions. Thus, today's outing.

"Troops start shipping out in a week," Bartz stated as he got out and pulled a five iron from his bag. "Active duty units first, then the reservists after we've gotten them up to speed. The base outside Muscat will be jammed with 200,000 people inside of 60 days, while their gear starts accumulating 600 miles west at Thumrait. I'm getting flak from the higher ups, but some good cover from the White House once I convinced them how much money could be saved doing it this way. Fewer airlift assets for Oman, more to bring the wetbacks up from Latin America. My bosses at the Pentagon can choke on it," Bartz concluded with a bitter chuckle.

He hit a crappy shot, hooking the ball left of the green and into the grass next to a lagoon.

"Hmmm. Wonder if it rolled in or stayed dry?" he asked himself.

"I wouldn't wade in to look for it if I were you," cautioned Hanrahan.

"Yeah? Why not?"

"The greens keeper told me the lagoons here are stocked with some sort of carnivorous fish. Says he buys rotten hamburger to feed them with. We'll have to ask Tikriti what species they are. He's part owner of this place, he told me. That's why we're getting as much free golf here as we want."

"Yeah, well I'm not rotten hamburger," Bartz shot back, returning to the cart and driving to the lagoon's edge. "I'm in luck anyway. Ball's caught on the lip, no harm, no foul. Perfect position for a lefty like me to pitch it on. So, how're things going on your end of this deal, Mack?"

Bartz found a crushed cookie in his pocket and hurled the handful of crumbs into the lagoon. They were instantly met by a flurry of strange looking, hyper-aggressive fish. "Christ! I guess the greens keeper wasn't bullshitting. I'll be real careful where I stand. Those things jumped more than a foot out of the water."

"My side of the deal is on track, too," said Hanrahan. "*Obama* Group's getting pulled off station immediately and coming home via the Pacific. Stopping in San Fran to join the *Roosevelt* in some sort of gay pride water parade under the Golden Gate Bridge and down the bay. Around the beginning of December, *Obama* goes into dry dock and *Roosevelt* starts ferrying refugees up from Central and South America. Won't be on station off of Oman until April or so."

"Gay pride water parade? Sounds sick, Mack. Bunch of degenerates flouncing around and celebrating their power over the U.S. Navy, as if our ships are their new bathtub toys. I wonder if Borgasma will be there urge them on."

"Who? Oh, the Secretary of F&A?"

"SecFAGO, you mean. Cil Borgasma. What kind of name is that? I've never been able to figure out if SecFAGO is a he or she," Bartz sneered.

"Who knows?" Hanrahan responded with a touch of impatience. "Anyway, everything's going as smoothly as we could have hoped."

"You trust that raghead, Tikriti?"

"No further than I can toss a grease rag."

"Me neither, Mack. I'll be real happy when this business is over and done with."

Bartz attempted to pitch the ball from beside the lagoon to the green and overshot, sending the ball into the lagoon on the other side. The water boiled for a moment before the fish realized the ball wasn't something they could eat.

"You can keep that one!" Bartz shouted at them, turning to Hanrahan. "Look at those fish climbing all over each other like a bunch of fucking faggots. I wouldn't touch that ball even if I could get it back."

Hanrahan couldn't wait for their round to be over. A little bit of Bartz went a long way. It was amazing the man had risen as far as he had. Their association couldn't end soon enough.

****

In 3rd Platoon's barracks at Fort Stewart, the troops were rising in the predawn darkness for early chow and a full morning of physical training. Many wondered why they had ever volunteered for military service, though not for long if they had time for introspection. For a few, the military was a calling. For many, it was a necessity in a nation with diminished employment prospects on the civilian side. The Oman call up jeopardized their civilian jobs and their family life, but at least offered the prospect of full employment at full pay, possibly tax free combat pay, during their expected year overseas. To take advantage of that opportunity, however, they had to measure up to the regular Army's physical requirements, and that was proving difficult for most. They were older, and definitely softer, than when they went through boot camp.

Sergeant Gonzales was no longer surprised that Lieutenant McIvor joined them every morning, such regular participation in PT uncommon for most officers, and she greeted her CO with a crisp salute. "Platoon's all accounted for, sir."

The term, "Ma'am," had been dropped as a form address for female military officers upon the demand of F&A, to be replaced by one form applicable to all. The Pentagon had been offered several alternatives, F&A Secretary Borgasma letting it be known there was a strong preference for the term "Mizra". The Joint Chiefs quickly defaulted to the sole traditional choice allowed them, "Sir", and stipulated severe penalties for use of the old term in order to mollify Borgasma.

In camo pants and T-shirt, McIvor returned the salute. "Is everybody here?"

"One in sick bay with flu, two out on doctors' notes with severe blistering from yesterday's PT."

"Where are they?"

"On barracks fire watch, sir."

"Can they walk?"

"More of a hobble, but they can get around," answered Gonzales.

"Get them out here. The barracks can watch itself."

"Private Martinez, fetch Poulter and Chao. Tell them they've got three minutes to report for PT with the Platoon."

Gonzales hoped this sort of thing wouldn't have negative repercussions for McIvor. She was starting to like the Lieutenant's forceful attitude and single-mindedness in getting 3rd Platoon up to speed. The weekend warriors were either going to get whipped into shape fast or fall by the wayside and face possible separation from the Army. Politics were sure to get involved in what should be a straightforward, unambiguous task. On the other hand, scuttlebutt had it Colonel Peters, who would soon be running Second Battalion, had the backs of her unit commanders. Time would quickly tell. They only had 40 days left to get it together before flying halfway around the world to Oman.

When the two limping privates joined the formation, Gonzales and McIvor led everyone on a brisk run through the pines. As they strung out along the trail, the fit ones pulled toward the front and others drifted back, struggling.

"Too many cigarettes, Chapa? Or was it chalupas?" chided the cocky, blond amateur boxer, Higgins, as she passed Chapa by.

"Fuck you, Paddy Wagon!," gasped Chapa.

Higgins dodged another slowing figure, a bulky, big-shouldered farm girl from Arkansas named Erickson and nicknamed for the U of A football team. "Big girls to the back, Razorback!" she taunted.

Razorback just laughed, good natured no matter the circumstance.

"Lay off, Higgins, or you can run this course again all by yourself," shouted Gonzales from in front.

Next to her, McIvor had slipped into that peculiar introspective place a long run could take you to. On the whole, she was pleased with the people she'd inherited. The contradictory dictates to push them hard while avoiding attrition provided plenty of stress, but the joy of finally attaining a line command more than offset any negatives. She'd find a way to bring them all along with Gonzales' help. She blessed her good fortune every day in having such a strong right hand. The Army hadn't given her much back until now, but she had to believe that was changing with this assignment and with these soldiers. It was all she had ever wanted since she was a little girl, to follow in her father's footsteps as an infantry commander.

"Let's pick up the pace on the home stretch, Sergeant. I think they can handle it."

Gonzales nodded in agreement.

"Move those feet faster, people! Extra watch duty for the last five in!"

****

In the world of finance, when demand outstripped supply, fevered minds found a way to increase that supply and generate the resultant profit. The Lone Star was not immune to this phenomenon.

The issued amount of the base currency, stuck at 30 billion LS, would in 70 days be followed by another half trillion Lone Stars as Kowloon's gold sitting in the Texas Depository in Round Rock became the unencumbered property of Texas and offsetting energy-backed bonds issued by Texas became the unencumbered property of Kowloon Holdings. The world wanted those half trillion Lone Stars now to hedge and speculate with as well as to carry out actual, "physical" transactions where Lone Star banknotes and electronic sums changed hands between corporations and financial institutions. Global banks began putting them into play in virtual form as WILS, meaning "when issued" Lone Stars. Swaps and other contracts called for delivery of WILS three months out or more, when a sufficient supply of new Lone Stars would be available to satisfy those deals. Through this bit of legerdemain, Lone Star futures and options exploded in volume to over ten trillion LS. The Lone Star rose to $1.04 from parity with the dollar at the time of its first issuance, during Judge Biermann's incarceration in the booze-filled safe room in Austin.

As activity and demand for the new currency picked up, lobbyists for those prohibited from participating, the U.S. banks and exchanges, screamed bloody murder to Congress, catching the leadership off guard. The White House had assured them the Lone Star would never be issued and if it somehow was, would collapse like some sort of ill-conceived Bitcoin knockoff.

Vance Carling had fielded angry calls from Senate Leader Kessel, Speaker Frankman, and many others from the other end of Pennsylvania Avenue, giving him an idea for how to handle the discussion about the Lone Star he'd been putting off with Palma.

"Can you assemble a small delegation to come see Palma with your concerns, Martin?" he asked the Speaker of the House. "I'll give the meeting priority."

Which really isn't your place, is it? Frankman said to himself, noting Carling's complete usurpation of Palma's chief of staff, a friend of Frankman's who officially controlled Palma's appointment book. Aloud, he answered, "I can do that, and coordinate with Kessel so we all come over together. I think that would be best, Carling."

"Agreed, Mr. Speaker," responded Carling, smoothly adjusting to Frankman's unfriendly tone and dropping use of his first name. "The president can see you at one this afternoon. I'll clear a full hour for you."

"Thank you so much, Carling. A whole hour," said Frankman sarcastically. "While you're tending to this matter, it would be a good idea to have Paul Jovian there, too. Can you manage that?"

Frankman's request caught Carling totally off guard. Why on earth would he want Jovian present? He quickly glanced at the calendar tracker on his Anjou smartphone, one that had been specially modified not to track *him*, and noted Jovian was in town today. "I think we can pull Paul off of the campaign trail if it's critical for him to attend your meeting, though the Lone Star is not in his area of expertise or responsibility. Can you tell me why you want him there?"

After a long and pregnant pause, Frankman responded, "Oh, I think you know why. We'll be at the Oval Office at one. It would also be really, really good if you could have Al Morse present in person or telephonically, too, if that's possible. We've missed him so much."

Frankman hung up and Carling slumped back in his chair. "Shit! Shit, shit, shit!" he exclaimed, suddenly realizing Blue Blood probably talked to Frankman as well as to Jovian, and that fool, Jovian, must have blathered to someone, probably Blue Blood on a subsequent call, that Carling was straightening Palma out on the Lone Star matter. Now, in front of everyone at the one o'clock meeting, the shit was going to hit fan as to why Carling hadn't told Palma about the change in policy being demanded by their corporate cronies. Carling tried to think of a way to mitigate things, but a zillion other tasks on the front burner this morning demanded his attention. One o'clock would be that rare meeting where Carling just had to let the chips fall.

****

Palma was feeling very laid back as the delegation filed into the Oval Office and filled the couches and chairs. He remained behind his desk appearing far more placid than normal. His personal physician had given him something to quiet the tick in his left cheek, and it had given him a slight buzz. Bourbon laced coffee all morning, with a pinch of white powder from his secret stash, had furthered its effect, and he liked it a lot. He hadn't felt this relaxed since taking the bow at the Democratic Convention in LA, nor this powerful and in control of things. He stared languidly at the assemblage, mildly surprised to see his political advisor, Paul Jovian, among them, since the topic du jour was supposed to be the Lone Star.

"No Al Morse with us today, so I see," observed Frankman drily.

"Al isn't doing meetings or phone calls these days," Palma drawled.

"Why not?" asked Senate Leader Kessel. "We're in the thick of the campaign, for heaven's sake."

"He's sick," stated Palma with a slight smile.

Carling stared at him. Something was very off. Palma had spent the last three weeks wound tighter than a watch. Now he almost seemed drugged.

Others were registering the weirdness as well, and there was an uncomfortable silence.

"Well," said Palma finally, "what'd you want?"

Frankman cleared his throat, giving Palma a hard stare. "A couple of things. First, I want to ask you point blank, and him…" he pointed to Paul Jovian, "where Morse is. We haven't seen him since LA and that's very troubling. If he's in a hospital somewhere, we need to know where and we need to know when he can have visitors. There are a lot of critical issues building up and we need his consultation."

"Like I said, Martin…" Palma trailed off and started doodling with his pen, defacing a fancy document on his desk, probably a treaty or something else of importance. "Like I said, Martin, he's sick. You'll have to settle for little old me."

Kessel stirred, uneasy. "Jay, we…mean no disrespect, but there are ongoing matters we've been working on with Al, matters we'd have to bring you up to speed on."

"Try me."

Frankman turned to Jovian. "Have *you* talked with Al lately?"

Jovian gave a negative shake of his head.

Carling watched everything, his mind running at warp speed. Was that why they wanted Jovian here, just to ask him face to face if he knew where the Vice President was and how he was doing. He was amazed they hadn't triggered one of Palma's tantrums with their pointed requests for access to Morse.

"Was the Lone Star just a pretext to get into my office this afternoon and ask me about Morse?" asked Palma mildly, with a lopsided smile.

"No, Jay," Kessel answered nervously, casting an imploring glance at Frankman. "No, the Lone Star is a very serious matter indeed. We really didn't expect to see it issued, but now that it has been, it seems to be attracting a lot of commercial interest."

"Take away their gold and you take away their ability to make trouble," Palma stated in slurred voice.

"What?" Frankman was all but scratching his head.

"Cut off the head of that snake down there," continued Palma in a voice barely audible, as he began doodling again. "…cut it off. Put it on a stick."

"Jay, I'm afraid I'm not following you," said Frankman. "Our friends in the banking and trading industries are crying foul because they're shut out of dealing in the Lone Star while their foreign competitors are cleaning up with it.

Palma doodled on in the thick, nervous silence, pursing his lips as if about to whistle. Suddenly he looked up sharply, as though startled they were all in the room and looking at him.

"Tell you what, gentlemen and ladies, let's revisit this soon. Appreciate you all stopping by like this. Grab a cookie on the way out, now."

He rose, prompting them all to their feet, and without further comment left.

Everyone turned to stare at Carling.

"What was that all about?" queried Kessel.

"That was about the fact that the president hasn't decided what to do about the Lone Star, that he wants you all to know that Al Morse isn't seeing anyone at this time, and that there are cookies on the sideboard out there. Good ones. They look like little windmills."

Frankman scowled at Carling, giving a disgusted grunt. "Well, this was a God damned waste of time."

Carling ushered the perturbed group out into the waiting room, happy that through a very strange set of circumstances he had dodged a major bullet, though concerned that he might have a major new problem. What the hell was going on with Palma?

****

The abortive Lone Star meeting had put Palma in a melancholy mood. He told Carling to cancel the rest of the day's appointments and accompany him on a trip across town in an unmarked vehicle, with unmarked Secret Service vehicles escorting them. They arrived at an unmarked, windowless, multi-story building with an underground garage. They rode an elevator to the top floor and were greeted by a white coated physician who led them down the hall. The Secret Service detail was left behind.

They entered a dimly lit room full of chemical smells and whirring pumps and motors. Cords and tubes ran across the tile floor to a stainless steel tube the size of a sarcophagus. Through a porthole in the top of it, they could see what was left of Al Morse, technically alive but long since brain dead. A mechanical heart circulated his artificial blood while motors pumped fluids that kept him hydrated. The steel sarcophagus, a barometric chamber, contained oxygen rich air at high pressure to suppress growth of the open wounds covering Morse's body, which seemed shrunken from when Carling had last seen it.

"We've got to keep him from going bad," said Palma quietly, his normally emotionless face softening with apparent sadness, stunning Carling, who wondered if Palma was ill. "We need him on stage with us when we declare victory on election night, and again at the inauguration."

"That's impossible!" responded Carling before he could help himself.

Palma turned to him, clapping his hands on Carling's shoulders.

"He's got to be up there with me, Vance. Legally, morally, spiritually, I've got to have him up there with me, whatever it takes, waving to the crowd."

"Uh…perhaps a stand in of some sort -"

Palma turned and pointed to the thing behind the porthole. "No! No, no, no. It's got to be Al himself. Up there, next to me. Figure out a way, Vance. Figure out a way…to make…"

Palma stared into the porthole, patting the tube, face quivering as though he was about to begin sobbing. Carling suddenly had the disconcerting image in his mind of Hitler tearing up like this in the bunker as the Russians closed in.

Palma turned to Carling with watery eyes and a bleak countenance. "Go on. Have the Secret Service take you back. I'll be here awhile."

Yes, Carling thought as he left the president alone with Morse and the hovering doctors. I've got a big problem brewing here, and getting Morse up on stage is the least of it.

6

Alice Tillinghast, the Under Secretary of the Treasury for Domestic Finance, had been shown the abyss and then the path to redemption. Two very powerful people had come into her office without notice and closed the door so their meeting would be undisturbed and unheard. Facing her were Vance Carling and Eduardo Montalban, Attorney General of the United States. Montalban quickly produced documents and made the case that Tillinghast would whither under scrutiny for her past tax evasions, and that the Department of Justice was armed with damning IRS evidence and would pursue charges if the matter couldn't be settled.

After twenty brutal minutes of this, the Attorney General wished her a good day and departed, leaving the woman thoroughly shaken and alone with Carling. Her past on Wall Street, as a colleague of Treasury Secretary Foster Hathaway when they worked at Goldman Sachs, had made her a lot of money and led her to engage in some very aggressive ploys to reduce her taxes. Everyone on Wall Street skated along the edge when it came to their taxes, because few ever fell under a microscope for it. She had made the mistake of entering high level government service at the behest of her old boss, raising her profile and drawing enemies she had not anticipated, and now she was well and truly caught.

"There's a way out of this mess," Carling offered.

She merely nodded, listening intently to whatever the special advisor to the president had to offer in the way of a solution. Willingness to be amenable was written all over her face.

Carling laid out the game plan. Replace the current Fiscal Assistant Secretary of the Treasury, Ricardo Montez, the person who actually controlled the federal government's accounts and trust funds, with one of his assistants, a minor functionary named Nathan Baum. Do it quietly, keeping Montez physically in place, coming to his office every day so he wouldn't arouse suspicion that he was in fact under investigation for major fraud. Give Baum a free hand to move money around without oversight or question. Tell Hathaway nothing about any of this. Go on as if nothing had changed.

"It's that simple," Carling said with a friendly smile. "Montez out, Baum in, with a free hand, and Hathaway none the wiser, since he's got his hands full with other matters and the president doesn't' want him distracted. Do it immediately, and quietly, and you won't be hearing from Justice or the IRS again. Can I report your cooperation in this matter back to President Palma when I see him this afternoon?"

"You most definitely can, Mr. Carling." Tillinghast couldn't keep the relief out of her voice. "Nathan Baum will be taking over from Ricardo Montez before this day is out."

"And Secretary Hathaway?"

"No need to distract him with minor personnel changes," she replied. "I know he's busy with so many other things."

"So pleased to hear it. The smoothness and efficiency of your operation here is a real credit to you, Ms. Tillinghast. The president has noticed and is very favorably impressed. Have you ever pondered that, down the road, you might want to consider serving at the Federal Reserve, on the Board of Governors? It would be an idea worth pondering."

Carling rose, shook hands, and wished her the very finest of days. After he left she closed the door, slumping into her chair as her hands began to shake and her knees turned rubbery, her emotions an overwhelming mix of fear, relief, guilt, and powerful glow of unbridled ambition.

****

Two days later Carling met with Nathan Baum deep in the Treasury Building in a large conference room converted to a bull pen. At half a dozen desks sat Baum's handpicked assistants, a group of geeky super accountants he called his "munchkins." Baum himself enjoyed the privacy of a glass walled office thrown up quickly while the bull pen was being assembled. His desk faced away from the pen at a wall covered with large, high definition computer screens on which were displayed spreadsheets and schematics of how money was flowing between accounts. Access to Baum's command center was strictly controlled, and no one, not even Alice Tillinghast, his immediate superior, could enter without his permission.

Baum was pasty, balding, short, and obese, his suit ample enough but his white shirt confining him like a tightly stuffed sausage casing. Carling found it uncomfortable to look at and diverted his eyes to the desktop, which was littered with candy wrappers and empty potato chip bags as well as stacks of reports and various compendia. Baum was bouncing in his chair with excess energy as he described his activities since taking over the federal government's checkbook. A pile of empty Monster and Red Bull cans in and around Baum's wastebasket caught Carling's eye before he focused on what the man was showing him.

"We've been doing a land office business in outbound wire transfers," Baum informed Carling excitedly. "Big bucks to the defense contractors, the Rightful Citizens Coalition, La Luz, etcetera, etcetera. Nearly half a trillion out the door since setting up in here yesterday morning, and that's just for your stuff , Mr. Carling. We've got all of the government's regular business to do, too."

"Call me Vance. We're going to be doing a lot of work together."

"Sure thing. After your projects, we've burned another 300 billion catching up on normal budget stuff that old Ricardo dropped the ball on. It's a damned good thing the Chinese bought all those bonds a few weeks ago. The way the bucks are going out, Vance, we'll need another deal like that one real soon. Of course, there're plenty of trust funds and Pentagon pools I can raid if I've got a totally free hand here."

"Totally free, Nathan," Carling assured him. "How are you covering all of these distributions so flags don't go up right and left, like for the Pentagon accounts for instance?"

"Across the board reclassification of accounts, something Secretary Hathaway himself started us on a few years ago. For instance, if I move ten billion out of the Pentagon's Oman deployment account and shift it to a bonus fund for federal employees, I classify the transaction as a capital investment, as though it was creating long term asset instead of vanishing into government workers' wallets. Capitalizing it like that keeps it from showing up in the operating budget as an expense. Instead, it shows up as a Pentagon asset called something like "interagency goodwill". A bit…well, a *lot* twisted in terms of rationale, but hey, it's nothing new these days. As long as it stays out of the operating budget, its invisible, and it's not like anybody's going to audit us, since *we're* the U. S. effing Treasury. Mess with us and we'll sick the IRS on you, know what I mean? Kind of like being God!"

Baum fished another can of Red Bull out of his desk and ripped the top off of it, sucking it down in three gulps and slam dunking the can into the wastebasket with a clatter as it hit all of the other empties.

"Sorry. Needed that! Hey, you want one?"

"No, I'm good, Nathan. Looks like you're on track. Is there anything else you need right now?"

"Not right now, but I gotta tell you, Vance, that we're burning money like a wildfire. In a couple months we're going need another few trillion, the way my cash flow model is shaping up. Tax revs aren't even going to cover a dime on the dollar of what's flying out of here in the next 90 days, not to mention the fact a lot of U.S. treasuries are coming due and the holders aren't showing signs of rolling their payouts into new treasuries. We gotta cover those payouts somehow if we can't convince the holders to roll them into new paper. I hope President Palma understands all this."

"The president understands and has plans in mind for dealing with the issues you're bringing up, though any ideas you have would be of great interest to the president. Meanwhile, just keep the dollars flowing the way we need for them to."

"I'm on it like white on rice, Vance! Me and my munchkins going 24/7 just so long as we've got plenty of Red Bull and Monster around!"

"I'll see to it that a truckload is delivered to you and your crew, compliments of the White House."

****

David Stoll and his attorney had been sitting in the waiting room of the IRS facility in Waco for nearly two hours, waiting to make their appeal to the agent who'd demanded their presence this day. Stoll had kept in touch with his office via cell phone, and his attorney had done the same with his law office, while cooling their heels and growing progressively angrier. Both were very busy individuals with much more productive ways to spend their time, but they dared not leave. Stoll found it more offensive than a doctor or dentist being tardy to see him, since he at least had the option of bailing out in those cases. A doctor or dentist could charge Stoll a no show penalty, but they couldn't threaten his livelihood or his family's security the way the IRS could. So he sat, knowing the attorney keeping him company had his meter running, making this whole proposition that much more stressful.

At the two hour mark, his attorney begged off citing he was due in court shortly.

"Try not to say much or answer too many questions, Dave. If it gets uncomfortable, ask to reschedule and don't be shy about citing the long wait today as the reason, but stay courteous. I'll call you as soon as I get out of the courtroom."

At last, just after the attorney left, a fat, sloppy looking black man in a short sleeved shirt and rumpled khakis shuffled toward Stoll, introducing himself as Kewan Jammel and offering the limpest of handshakes while emanating an aura of jaded hostility.

"Follow me," he said, leading Stoll down a sterile hallway to a small, windowless office that seemed more like an interrogation room. Indeed, the lack of personal items seemed to confirm that the room was not Jammel's regular office. Stoll sat on a metal folding chair while Jammel dropped his bulk into a padded executive armchair with a sigh. There was a thick accordion file on the desk from which Jammel withdrew a document on IRS letterhead, along with another on Department of Fairness and Affirmation in Gender Outcomes letterhead.

The government had spent serious money on logo design, colored inks, and high quality rag paper, Stoll noted. As a small business owner, he was attuned to such excesses and avoided them out of financial necessity. The federal government seemed to have no such restraint in the matter of its document stock or much else, and it made Stoll wonder just how plush Jammel's actual office was. New and recently renovated federal facilities, to Stoll's observation, had become quite upscale with deep carpeting, wood paneled walls, fancy artwork, and recessed lighting. Many federal complexes contained restaurants, shops, and gyms, and offices with furniture that would do credit to the executive wing of a Fortune 500 company.

"The reason you here, Mr. Stool, is that -"

"It's Stoll, Mr. Jammel. It rhymes with stole, like someone stole something," Stoll chuckled.

Jammel stared back without humor a long moment, then gestured to the IRS document. "Mr….Stoll, this is serious. You in violation of federal law here. That's why the freeze on the bank."

"I know this is serious, but I have no idea why, nor where this is all coming from," Stoll responded, trying to keep his cool. He'd been denied access to his bank account for a week and he was beginning to panic. Payroll was due. He'd taken up the matter with an IRS taxpayer advocate and gotten nowhere. Then he had received Jammel's summons yesterday demanding he show up at a specific time today, which was now over two hours ago.

"Why was my account frozen? To my knowledge I am fully current on my tax filings and payments."

Jammel pointed to the other document on his desk. "This F&A complaint was ignored, so they institute a fine which you also ignore."

"I've never received anything from the…the F&A."

"Their records say you did."

"Can they produce a certified mail receipt or something like that, because I've never received anything from them."

"That's a problem for you, unless you can prove you didn't get their letter."

"Prove I didn't get a letter? How would I be able to prove something I *didn't* get? Look, what was their complaint about."

"You have a Billy Mon-row work for you?"

"Billy Monroe? Yeah, he worked on my production line until he showed up one day in a dress."

"And then you fired him."

"No, I told him not to dress like that on the floor. It's dangerous. The women working on the line don't dress that way for that reason. If an OSHA inspector dropped in and saw that, I'd be looking at a safety violation and a big, fat fine," Stoll explained. "Anyway, Monroe quit the next day, no reason given. I never heard from him again."

"Not what he say, Mr….Stoll. His complaint to F&A say you belittle him, harass him, and call him gay names. When you never respond to F&A, the fine get issued. When you ignore that, we required to enforce it."

"How much was this fine I never heard about?"

Jammel furrowed his brow, lips moving silently as he read the document. "It be for $25,000, doubled for lack of response twice before coming here, where it double again statutory."

"I didn't quite understand, Mr. Jammel. Exactly how much are we talking about at this time?"

"Two hundred grand."

Stoll was stunned and speechless.

He'd grown up on a struggling farm that was mortgaged and eventually lost, and swore he'd never go through the experience again. It had driven him to excel in school and earn a scholarship to Iowa State where he graduated with a degree in mechanical engineering. After jobs at two large corporations that ended in layoffs, where he was first forced to train his own replacements who'd been shipped in from third world countries, he decided the safest job would be one he created for himself. Stuck in Austin after the second layoff, he borrowed heavily to attend the University of Texas and earn an MBA while Sharon, his young wife, found part time work in a law office.

The gamble had paid off. Stoll partnered with small contract manufacturer in Round Rock whose son he'd attended UT Austin with, finding business, managing product runs, and eventually earning his equity position on sweat and smarts. When the owner decided to retire, he sold his interest to Stoll, taking Stoll's guarantee on a seller's note. Stoll worked harder than he ever had, sometimes a hundred hours a week. Sharon saw little of him but they still managed to buy a house and bring two children into the world. She gave up her law firm job to raise them.

The business remained small and nimble, never more than fifteen people on the payroll, because work could be terribly unpredictable and keeping costs down was the only way to weather the dry spells. Stoll kept a rainy day reserve in the bank and paid himself last after his employees and the business got what they needed. In the past year, he'd drawn $75,000 out to live on, the most ever, and with Sharon's fierce economizing at home, they'd managed to exist comfortably though without many frills. Vacation was a long weekend off once a year, renting a cabin in the east Texas pines or tent camping in Big Bend out west.

Now, Stoll faced ruin. In total shock, he struggled to form a coherent thought.

Kewan Jammel looked at Stoll without pity, and in fact with resentment. Here in front of him was another lifelong beneficiary of white privilege, one of life's lottery winners who thought he could step on people like Billy Monroe and get away with it. Not this time. Not on Jammel's watch. He would throw the book at this cracker and happily watch his snowflake ass sink under the waves.

Jammel, who had barely completed his GED and never finished his associate degree, had only gotten on board with the IRS because his daddy had once worked there. He had eighteen years in and just another twelve to go before drawing a fat pension. A full work week was only 35 hours anymore thanks to the treasury employees union, and Jammel was paid a salary of $125,000 a year with health, pension, and other benefits worth another $50,000. He took five weeks of vacation annually, usually hitting top resorts in the Caribbean or the big casinos in Vegas. He hadn't had a significant raise in two years and was getting very angry about it. His 5,000 square foot house, three SUVs, and power boat cost a lot to keep, and servicing all those loans kept him tapped out. This creep sitting in front of him probably supported the kind of politicians who fought raises for federal workers. Well, what goes around comes around.

"I give you one week pay the fine, or we start seizing stuff and selling it, including your business assets, your house, your cars, and your pension fund."

Stoll gave a bitter laugh. "Pension fund? Now there's a luxury I've never been able to afford."

7

Late October was unseasonably hot in Georgia, hitting the 90s in the afternoon as Razorback Erickson struggled to reassemble her M240 machine gun and shove in the clip before Sergeant Gonzales blew her whistle. Razorback didn't quite make it, but she was closer than she'd ever been.

"You just got overrun, Erickson!" the sergeant yelled. "Higgins, Poulter, Rodriguez, you're all dead!"

They looked up, covered in sweat with the sun beating down, M16s still not fully assembled and ready to fire.

"Some shade wouldn't hurt, Sarge," Poulter suggested.

"You won't find any shade in Oman, and the temps make Georgia seem downright frosty. Break 'em apart, ladies. Parts on the ground."

Amidst muted cursing and grumbling, they broke down their weapons for the umpteenth time. They'd begun to harden up from all the PT, and now the emphasis of their day had shifted to honing their weapons proficiency. Gonzales was impressed at their progress but concerned about the deployment, which was only three weeks off. They wouldn't be anywhere near combat ready before flying out, but with luck they'd have time to get up to speed after settling in over there, before anything could pop.

They'd lost three people to the rigors of the conditioning regimen, which wasn't bad compared to most units. With luck, they'd deploy with 53 people including herself and McIvor, putting their strength at a respectable 95%. Morale was excellent, as was her interaction with the lieutenant. You could never be ready enough, though, when you were heading into the land of the bad guys.

Gonzales held up her stopwatch. "On my mark…go!"

The desperate scramble began anew.

"Belay all that muttering and get it done!" she shouted at them.

****

Longstreet met with the governors of New Mexico and Arizona at the municipal airport in Marfa and ferried them up to his ranch in the Davis Mountains, located on the northern side of Mount Livermore. Desert gave way to pinion pine and juniper, and eventually, as they neared an elevation of eight thousand feet, to a forest of ponderosa pine and aspen rare in this region.

"How big is your spread?" asked Anna Koors, the Arizona governor.

"We've got 16,000 acres, about a third of it in the mountains and well-watered, so you'll see cattle wandering here and there." Longstreet looked relaxed in jeans, cowboy boots, and a striped shirt with pearly snaps. "I have my great, great granddaddy to thank for it. He came out after the War of Northern Aggression when the army was still fighting the Apaches. Land was cheap for those willing to risk their scalps."

They topped a ridge and dropped toward the head of a heavily timbered canyon where the road ended in a clearing. Adjacent was a rustic structure of stone and log tucked into the shade of the pines, built into the face of the cliff formed by the canyon's headwall.

"And I have my granddaddy to thank for this place," Longstreet said. "When he cleared pasture down the canyon near the springs, he hauled ponderosa trunks up here to frame this lodge and plank the floors. My wife oversaw renovation of it a few years ago, so I hope you'll find it comfortable. Here she is…"

Anita Longstreet met them on the porch, a smiling woman of about fifty with a dark complexion and streaks of gray accenting long, dark hair. Koors was surprised and didn't hide it well enough, because the New Mexico governor, Berto Arguello, walking beside her, whispered "Anita Longstreet nee Baca. Yes, she's Hispanic."

"I didn't know that," she whispered back. "Not what I would expect, given his stance on closing the border."

"Longstreet has a lot of support among residents of Texas who happen to be Hispanic. They want the border under control, too," Arguello replied.

Next to Mrs. Longstreet stood a distinguished, gray haired man in a golf shirt and khakis. Wyatt Brady, the CEO of Kinder Morgan, the company whose CO2 pipeline had blown up a month ago near Pecos, was known to all three governors. His company was a major employer and taxpayer in all three states and there were warm handshakes all around.

"Let me show you to your rooms," Mrs. Longstreet said, inviting them into the Lobby-like main room. A lacquered pine floor covered with cowhide rugs spread out under a vaulted ceiling held up by girders made of entire tree trunks. The north side of the room looked through French doors and across a flagstone patio to a lofty view of the canyon falling away, slopes hidden by dense forest.

Thirty minutes later they gathered on the patio under the shade of three ancient ponderosas growing out of openings left in the stonework when the patio was built. Their resin scented the early evening air along with the smell of steaks on the grill overseen by a greybeard in a battered cowboy hat. He also served as bartender, fishing out beer and soft drinks, and mixing cocktails. The party eventually took seats around a plank table and enjoyed a feast of T-bones, baked potatoes, slaw, and beans, with cornbread on the side and peach cobbler for dessert.

Over coffee, Governor Koors sat back regarding her hosts. "This lodge of yours looks like it grew out of the mountain side, like it's been here forever, but I guess your family's been here forever."

"My ancestor showed up in these parts in the late 1860s," Longstreet responded, "but he was a newcomer compared to Anita's family."

"Oh?"

"My family settled in El Paso during the Pueblo Revolt, having fled Santa Fe," Mrs. Longstreet said shyly.

"That would've been in 1680," Governor Arguello exclaimed. "And do you know when your family first moved to Santa Fe, Anita?"

She laughed, pleased at his interest, "We do know that, thanks to the old family Bible that has all but disintegrated. We know they came up from Mexico in the original group led by Juan de Onate, to establish the first settlement ever in Nuevo Mexico."

Arguello stood and gave an elegant bow. "1598 that would be. I am honored to be in your presence, Senora Longstreet-Baca. Your family is ancient indeed. To think they were in New Mexico twelve years before Santa Fe itself came to exist."

"And 9 years before Jamestown was settled in Virginia, supposedly America's earliest settlement," Longstreet added.

"Do you take issue with your husband's stance on the border, Anita?" Koors asked.

"His stance?"

"You know, closing it down. Keeping the Latino immigrants from coming over."

"No, Anna, I don't take issue with his stance, I applaud it."

"That just strikes me as strange," Koors persisted.

"No more strange than keeping people from moving into your backyard and taking it over, Anna. Do you know what happens to nations that let themselves be overrun? Do you know of the Rhine River in 406 A.D.?"

"The Rhine? In Europe?"

"Yes, Anna, the Rhine in Europe. In 406 it froze solid and the barbarians came across into the Roman Empire, thousands, maybe millions of them. Rome failed to stop the migration and 70 years later the empire no longer existed."

"And you think this is like that?"

"This is worse than that, because our own government in Washington is inviting these new barbarians in to commit violence and steal jobs and votes. If we don't' stop it soon, and it is already almost too late, they will displace our culture with their corrupt one. No, I pray to God every day that my husband and others will rally the people to stop this terrible thing."

Mr. Longstreet paused and seemed to become self-conscious again, rising to her feet quickly followed by her guests. "Forgive my passion, please. You have much of importance to discuss among you and I shall bid you all a good night."

Indeed, it had grown dark and the air had begun to cool.

"Let's retreat inside by the fireplace," Longstreet suggested.

When he had them relocated to leather chairs in front of the cheery blaze, he began the business of the get together. "Our three states, and Wyatt's company, have been taking it on the chin since Palma shut down CO2 transmission lines across the country. We've seen a plunge in oil and gas production, shuttered refineries, and huge layoffs, all on the most specious of reasoning. In Texas, we suspect it all has to do with Palma's politics and nothing to do with the facts. Kinder Morgan has conducted an in-depth inspection of its pipelines and an investigation into what happened at Pecos. Wyatt?"

"Yeah, Jeff, we've been over every foot of pipe, every compressor, and every point of control along the Pecos pipeline and the rest. Except for minor corrosion that we'd be addressing in the normal course of business long before it's a problem, our transmission network gets a clean bill of health. At the Pecos site, we've got plenty of evidence suggesting sabotage, including explosive residue on the fragments we recovered. We've documented it all very carefully, everything from the safe condition of our network to the evidence Pecos was a deliberate act of destruction by someone, documentation I'll provide each of you. It's no secret that this shutdown is hurting us badly, and we're willing to fight back against the feds if you'll stand with us."

"How do you mean, Wyatt?" asked Arguello.

"I mean that if you are willing to let us resume operations in your states, we'll do so. We'll be fined by the feds for every day we flow CO2, but we'll fight those fines as well as the closure order itself all the way to the Supreme Court if we have to. However, our resumption will be short lived if you don't stand with us, both legally and, to be blunt, tactically."

"Tactically?" asked Koors.

"What Wyatt means by that," explained Longstreet, "is that we three states will provide for the security of the pipelines and prevent the feds from coming in and shutting off the flow. All three of us would have to act in concert since the CO2 originates in Arizona and the pipe runs across New Mexico and Texas."

"How would we stop the feds from messing with Kinder Morgan's pipeline or any other pipeline?" asked a skeptical Koors.

"With troops, or cops, or any other security force at your disposal," Longstreet stated.

The other two governors pondered this in silence.

Longstreet continued, "In Texas we're willing to station units of the State Guard along the pipe all the way from Pecos to Midland-Odessa, the Eagle Ford, and on to Houston."

"But, Jeff, what will your Guard do if federal agents show up with a court order to shut down the pipe?" asked a perturbed Arguello.

"We'll tell them no, Berto."

"And if a no won't stop them?"

"I'll arrest them and throw them in jail. And if they send more I'll arrest them, too."

They regarded him with faces full of doubt.

"Arizona has been a whipping boy for the feds since the days of Jan Brewer and Joe Arpaio," Koors complained. "We got badly beaten up for trying to enforce federal immigration law when the feds wouldn't do it themselves. You remember how that turned out. I'm not sure we have the stomach in my state for another knock-down, drag-out with Washington."

"Think carefully," Longstreet urged. "We are all hurting badly and it's only been a month. Palma's talking about a shutdown of six months, a year, or more. If your states will join forces with mine on this, Texas will bear the lion's share of the legal costs and provide you with some of our security forces if you need them. If we form a united front with Wyatt's company, we can get oil and gas production going again and put people back to work. If we don't, it's going to get very, very ugly, as in economic depression ugly. The feds are bullies. Confront them with firm resolve and they'll back off."

"Let's sleep on it," Wyatt suggested.

"Yes," agreed Arguello, "let us adjourn until morning, though I must say I have thought this through. It is very unjust. We have massive unemployment in our east, around Hobbs and Lovington, and also up in the San Juan Basin. The loss of energy tax revenue is hitting us hard. New Mexico will suffer seriously if it goes on much longer. Your offer of help, Jeff, inclines me to your view. Let me consider it further and give you an answer after the sun has risen."

Koors, still skeptical but willing to consider joint action, made unanimous their decision to call it a night.

In the morning, over breakfast out on the patio as the blue jays and the crows taunted each other in the treetops, they agreed the time had come to push back forcefully against Washington's overreach and restore their states' economic fortunes.

8

"You're requiring we keep a hundred billion of the next Lone Star issuance available for retail customers?" Abner Furlong asked Longstreet when he finally got through to the governor at his ranch in the Davis Mountains. He wasn't happy.

"That's right, Abner. Can't have you lending it all out to Barclay's and Deutsche Bank. It's the currency of Texas, and you'll have to keep a little of it on hand for Texans."

"Sounds like a lot, over 3,000 LS for every man, woman, and child in the state."

"How much of the original issue went to retail customers last month?"

"Off the top of my head? I'm not sure exactly."

"I am. It was only 2.7 billion of the 30 billion issue, Abner, from the Depository's own report, and people are mad about the fact they can't get their hands on a decent amount."

"Well, the shortage hasn't hurt the Lone Star's price. Sitting at a buck five as we talk."

"That's fine, but we're going to let the little guy in for a bigger piece of the action next time around. What else have you got going on?"

"I'm getting reports from security at the Depository that a lot of fed types have been hanging around the fence, snapping pictures and watching the Guard battalion. One of them launched a drone but the Guard brought it down with one shot. Told the guy he wasn't getting it back and that he'd be arrested if he tried it again. He vanished after that."

"Hearing anything from your Washington sources?"

"Not much. Seems like they've dropped their opposition for now. Nothing going on with Biermann. It might just be that they're distracted with the election so near at hand."

"Suits me. We're going to have our own distraction soon. Kinder Morgan's going to start flowing CO2 again in a few days, and the Texas State Guard will be providing security and, if necessary, interdiction. Koors and Arguello are onboard. Things could get real interesting real fast."

"I'm glad that sort of thing is beyond my purview, Jeff. I've got my hands full with the Lone Star. Only six more weeks until the mega tranche. It'll be fun watching the banks and brokers scrambling to settle all those 'when issued' transactions. There may be more 'when issueds' out there than there are Lone Stars to satisfy them."

"Just keep the whole thing from blowing up on us."

"Before you go, Jeff, what's going on down in Clingman?"

"Nothing good from the sound of it. Kowloon has moved in a couple thousand people as far as anyone can tell, and they're using their own contractors from China to construct a compound on top of Mesa de los Muertos. They've already built a road up onto it and a transmission line tapping into our main grid. What have you heard?"

"A banker friend in Alpine says the construction convoys are running in and out day and night and tearing up the highways something fierce. His brother is the park supervisor for Big Bend and he's up in arms about what it's doing to the tourist traffic. Said when he complained to HQ in DC, he got a call from the White House telling him to back off and shut up. The people in Clingman are livid because they've been crowded off their streets by constant traffic and their wells are going dry. Apparently Kowloon has punched new wells into the ground upstream on the Triple M, right where the owner's house used to stand before it burned down with him inside. Sounds like wholesale disregard of our laws and regulations going on down there."

"The whole thing stinks, Abner, and we're trying to find out what we can. Unfortunately, Kowloon is our biggest creditor thanks to the energy-for-gold deal. When you owe someone half a trillion dollars it's a good idea not to step on their toes if you can help it. Forgive me if I'm a bit paranoid about anything that might derail our bond deal and suck 3,750 tons of gold back out of the Depository. When that deal is finally put to bed in six weeks, we'll step up our investigation and get to the bottom of this Clingman situation.

****

"We can't wait any longer," the captain of the *U.S.S. Eisenhower* told CF7, the commander of the Seventh Fleet. "We've been deployed most of the last 15 months and putting off everything we could, but it's been building up. Now, we seem to have a problem with one of our shaft bearings and the seal on another. We've been taking water and running the pumps constantly but now those are wearing out. You told me to let you know when it was time for dry dock. It's time."

On the other end of the call, Vice Admiral Gillen, aka CF7, cursed for the thousandth time the Palma Administration's early retirement of half the Navy's *Nimitz* Class carriers. *Eisenhower* should have been switching off with *Reagan*, but *Reagan* had been mothballed. Instead, *Eisenhower* had no relief and had finally been run into the ground. Now, once the big ship went into dry dock in Yokosuka, it wouldn't be coming back out for six months or more, leaving Seventh Fleet without a carrier strike group, something that hadn't happened since the Seventh was created during World War Two.

"OK, captain. I'll get a nice dry spot ready for you to perch in. Say goodbye to your crew and let them know reassignments will be coming soon."

He rung off and looked out his window at the expansive Yokosuka naval base begun by the Japanese in 1871 in response to the visit of U.S. Commodore Mathew Perry's fleet of "black ships" eighteen years earlier. The Americans had taken it over as a prize of war in 1945 and it had grown immense. Tokyo was only 30 miles away.

Gillen reflected on the fact that the Navy was now down to two active aircraft carriers with *Eisenhower* being sidelined, two others stuck in long term overhauls, and the new *JFK* still not close to being delivered. The *Obama* had already left station in the Arabian Sea, steaming home across two Oceans to San Francisco, leaving the Persian Gulf region wide open for trouble. The *Roosevelt* wouldn't reach the Gulf until June or July of the coming year. It was a sad and alarming state of affairs but Gillen had long since tired of worrying about it since there was nothing he could do. Happily, his retirement was less than a year away.

****

Carling picked up the call from Nathan Baum.

"Vance," said the high pitched and perpetually breathless voice, "hate to bother you but we're going need some more cash soon."

"What are you talking about? You had 2.5 trillion dollars to work with when you took over last month, from the special bond issue we floated to the Chinese."

"Yeah, I know, but we've been forced to spend more than we planned paying off all of the treasuries coming due."

"How can that be, Nathan? The Chinese also agreed as part of our deal to roll all of their maturing treasuries into new ones."

"They've been doing that for sure, sopping up a lot of what we're auctioning, but it seems like they're the only ones buying U.S. paper besides the Fed. The Japs, Russians, Arabs…looks like they're walking away with their proceeds and putting them elsewhere. Result, we're losing altitude fast. Pretty soon Hathaway's going to notice, if he hasn't already. I can't keep things looking all smooth and nice much longer. We need fresh cash."

"How much more fresh cash, Nathan?" Carling asked, incredulous that 2.5 trillion dollars could vanish so quickly. He was starting to have doubts about Baum's competence, and maybe his honesty.

"Another half tril would see us to New Year's Day…maybe. These election expenses have been vaporizing money faster than a natural gas flare at a refinery. And the drop off in rollovers could really screw us if it picks up steam. Seems like nobody loves us anymore, or at least our T-bills."

"500 billion?" Carling was alarmed. "You need it when?"

"In two weeks, outside."

"Why did you wait until now to say something, Nathan?"

"Uh…we kinda got ahead of our bookkeeping for a while, focusing on all of these transfers and disbursements you wanted done. When the dust settled and we crunched our latest position, we realized the tank is about to run dry."

"This is insane!" Carling blurted in a rare loss of self-control, his throat tightening. Palma would go ape shit if he found about this, yet how could something this big and bad be hidden from him for long?

"Yeah, it's been real crazy around here, Vance. I've got an idea of something we could do, though. It would let us skate our way through the next couple of months if the rollover deficit doesn't get worse. You'd have to let me take control over Social Security."

"Social Security? The trust fund?"

"Nah. The trust fund's almost tapped out. I've got something else in mind."

"What?"

Baum explained. Carling couldn't believe his ears.

"This is too big a decision for you or me to make, Nathan. I want you to explain your idea to the president himself, after you've shown him a flow chart of what happened to 2.5 trillion dollars over one short month. I'll get back as to when."

****

The president was appalled when Carling explained that the federal government was nearly out of cash. Gone was the strange placidity of the past few weeks, and Palma's left cheek twitched with increasing violence as Carling laid out the situation.

"This can't be, Vance. We cleaned out the cupboards to raise that 2.5 trillion, and it was more than enough to take us into next year and the inauguration."

"We didn't know people would start a wholesale flight from U.S. treasuries, and it would be a lot worse if we hadn't negotiated that the Chinese roll their maturing paper over until after the election."

Carling decided to stick with Baum's main excuse, the lack of treasury rollovers. It would only make Palma apoplectic to point out that the election itself had become much more expensive than planned as Palma's standing with voters dropped, thanks in large part to the absence of Al Morse. In the vacuum of that, the inherent negative feelings of voters toward Palma had developed into a serious gravitational pull that Paul Jovian could only overcome with another huge cash infusion. Palma's approval rating was barely 30%, and Jovian requested another 100 billion from Carling to offset the damage. That kind of money simply wasn't to be had quickly except from one place, and Carling had thanked his stars that Baum was in place at the Treasury to accommodate him. He and Jovian had kept the matter between them.

For his part, Palma suspected he wasn't being shown the entire picture. This sort of bullshit so close to the election was unacceptable. If they could just keep a lid on for two more weeks he'd be reelected and able to exercise the awesome new power of the EOA, the Executive Orders Act, giving him greater power than Congress itself to enact new laws. Then he'd show everyone who was in charge.

He rubbed his hands together, trying to keep from massaging his quivering cheek. It wouldn't do any good anyway. He'd have to go back on that stuff he'd used earlier for it, even though it altered his mood more than he though prudent.

"So, what's the plan, Vance? Obviously we can't hit the wall just before Election Day."

"Baum, our man at Treasury, has something that could work, but it has a major downside."

"Isn't Baum the one that let this thing go to the last moment before telling us?"

"There are valid reasons for that, not that I'm happy about it. I've got him waiting outside if you want to hear his idea."

"That, and I want him to explain how things got this fucked up."

"He'll address that part of it, too. I'll get him."

Baum's physical appearance didn't impress Palma, nor did his hyper demeanor. Baum gave a nervous thumbnail sketch of where all the cash had gone while Palma listened without comment or question, but he didn't appear to be buying Baum's explanation.

"That was far too much money to vanish that quickly, Mr. Baum. I trust your records will bear scrutiny if I have the Office of Management and Budget look into them."

"We're still playing catch up on the records, so I hope the OMB will give us some breathing room. We've moved more money around quicker than anyone ever has in human history, and there're only seven of us to do it. Recordkeeping got behind the curve."

"Why so few people in your operation?"

"Vance said to keep it tight, as few as possible to minimize any leaks."

"I can't argue with that logic," said Palma begrudgingly. "What's your plan for coming up with 500 billion dollars over the next two months?"

When he heard the plan, Palma's estimation of Baum rose dramatically. Not that the plan wouldn't cause a political firestorm, but if the timing was right and they could hold off until they were past the election, Palma didn't care. In fact, he would enjoy wounding a constituency that had been a thorn in his side for years.

"We can do that," he told Baum, "as long as it isn't until after Election Day. I'm hearing we may run out of cash before then. What can you do to bridge us past the election?"

"We'll just delay payment on some bills, Mr. President, ones that won't upset anyone before they vote."

"Be sure of that, Mr. Baum."

****

David Stoll sat in the courtroom of Judge Biermann beside his attorney, and across from Kewan Jammel and an attorney from the IRS. Obtaining this hearing had cost Stoll dearly, eating a deep hole into his few unfrozen assets. His brother-in-law had purchased an unregistered car Stoll had been storing in a friend's unused garage, an extremely valuable collectible he'd purchased as an investment and that he'd intended to restore when he could find the time. His brother had paid him cash in the form of 50,000 Lone Stars, of which 20,000 went for legal costs and the rest into a duffel bag to meet his family's living expenses.

His attorney had used a little known procedural approach to move the hearing out of tax court, where their chances would be minimal, and into federal district court where they should, theoretically, have a chance of an early and possibly favorable pre-trial ruling. Taking the matter all the way to trial was beyond his diminished financial capacity, so today was an all-or-nothing play.

He was teetering on the brink, his business shuttered and his crew laid off. His business assets, nearly all of them leased, would soon go back to their owners if he couldn't resume operations. He was no longer making mortgage payments on his house and the wheels of foreclosure had begun to turn. His cars had been repossessed and he was making do with a car from a rent-a-wreck place that accepted weekly cash payments and didn't require a credit card.

If it went well today, and he got the IRS liens lifted and his bank accounts unfrozen, he believed he could still pull things back together. If not, he had tried his best against a loaded deck. He found himself mentally numb these days, unable to understand how this had happened and barely able to cope with day to day demands. At least Sharon didn't blame him, and she and the kids were solidly behind him.

The judge looked old and mean to Stoll as the sides presented their cases, Stoll's attorney stating the situation was a mistake caused by a lack of communication and through no fault of Stoll, who had acted properly throughout, while the IRS attorney argued it was a straightforward case of flaunting the rules and a deliberate failure to pay the resultant fine. Not once did Biermann, obviously bored and tired, look Stoll's way to assess him as a person.

"Everybody finished?" Biermann snapped after the IRS attorney sat back down.

Stoll's attorney stood again. "I have some additional comments on my client's character and his family's hardships as he struggles with this misplaced-"

"Enough," Biermann growled with a dismissive wave of his hand. "This matter more properly belongs in tax court, but since you brought it in here for a preliminary ruling, I'll provide you with one. F&A rules, which exist to protect a vulnerable and oft persecuted element of our society, were clearly violated by Mr. Stoll, and the fine properly assessed. Mr. Stoll's claim not to have received timely notices regarding the F&A's investigation and the subsequent assessment of the fine is hearsay, while F&A records state that the notices were in fact mailed. The IRS acted as it should have in enforcing the F&A's penalty by enforcing the fine and imposing further penalties as provided by law."

Biermann paused to take a sip of water. He'd felt thirsty ever since his safe room ordeal, and his throat dried out more quickly than it used to. Dipshit little hearings like this had become an annoyance and he thought often about tossing in his robe and turning his attention to the land empire he'd secretly accumulated during his judicial career. His 74,000 acre slice of the Triple M Ranch, for instance, was being torn up and abused by the Chinese, who'd drilled wells and built equipment yards and roads on his part of that dismembered property. He needed to get down there and straighten those bastards out. All they had was a right of way up to the mesa where their mining compound was located, not license to tear up his piece of the historic ranch. Maybe he could get them to buy it from him for a huge markup. Some of those rare earth deposits probably underlay his acreage, too, and not just the mesa.

"I find for the F&A and the IRS on all counts, and award them full recovery of their legal and administrative costs pursuant to this hearing. Mr. Stoll's claims, in full, are summarily dismissed with prejudice. This ruling is stayed pending trail, to take immediate effect should a timely trial not be pursued as per applicable filing deadlines. Adjourned."

The judge promptly vanished while Stoll's attorney held a quick pow wow with his IRS counterpart and Kewan Jammel. Stoll sat and watched it all in a daze until his attorney came back.

"I can't get them to budge on the 24 hour deadline for payment of the fine and the penalties, Dave, and the clock starting ticking when the Judge adjourned. I'm sorry. If you were a huge corporation we could file immediately for trial and keep fighting, but I'm afraid this is the end of the line for you and me. They want me to account for my fee and how you paid it, which is a not so subtle way of them saying my future fees are subject to seizure. My firm didn't even want me at this hearing, but you and I go back. My final advice is that you think about moving to Canada or someplace where the government regulators haven't become so overwhelmingly powerful and, frankly, tyrannical. If you stay in the U.S., try to find gainful employment in the 'gig economy', something that pays in cash. I can't ethically advise you not to report cash income, but merely point out that if you do, the IRS will likely seize it. You're a smart, hard-working guy, Dave, and I know you'll figure a way forward. Good luck to you and your family."

They shook hands and after the attorney made a quick retreat, Stoll found himself alone in the big room, facing a future emptier than this space, and all because he had allegedly hurt the feelings of a male production line worker who decided one day to show up in a dress and work around dangerous machinery. He now believed the rumors he'd been hearing about the F&A for years, that the F&A staged incidents at small businesses in order create a climate of terror and quick capitulation among the entrepreneurial class, a group the federal government and their corporate cronies wanted to drive out of existence. Maybe he *should* look into moving to Canada in order to start over.

9

Carling brought Paul Jovian in to help him talk Palma out of doing anything rash. They needed as little controversy as possible with the election a week away. Palma's approval had dropped into the 20s in most polls, and no one had ever been elected to the White House with anything approaching the president's negativity ratings. He was in freefall, and that was with an opponent who on the Republican side who almost didn't exist in the public mind. Most voters would pick an empty chair over Palma.

It fed Jovian's sense that there wouldn't be many elections allowed after this one, because the polls revealed an across-the-board detestation of the DC establishment and the federal government itself. People were sick of it, and afraid of where it was taking them. A citizenry with such attitudes couldn't be trusted to leave the DC status quo in place unless they no longer had the power to remove it by voting.

Invading the oil patch in Texas, New Mexico, and Arizona with federal storm troopers would make things all the harder, especially when those states had deployed massive security of their own to the critical areas. There could very well be violence if the feds moved in forcefully. Palma's reelection chances were narrow enough without sparking deliberate trouble and negative headlines.

"But they resumed operation of those pipelines in open defiance of us," Palma complained. "We need to slam them hard and shut it all back down."

"Which we can do through the court system, Jay," Jovian countered.

"That's too damned slow! They'll have production back up and running and undo the squeeze we've been putting on them. More important, we can't just allow such flagrant disregard of federal authority. It's unprecedented."

"Well, not exactly, Jay. Pot has been legal in Colorado, Washington, and a bunch of other states in violation of federal law for 16 years now, and we haven't done anything about it."

"That's not like this situation. It's not a public safety issue," Palma retorted.

"Some would argue otherwise."

"Tell you what, Paul. I'll sit back and cool my jets until after the election, and then I'm sending in the storm troopers as you call them. Longstreet doesn't get to defy us like this. It's bad enough when he acts on his own like he did with the Lone Star, but now he's getting other governors to join him in civil disobedience. It could catch fire and spread to other states. We can't have it."

"That's fine, Jay," Jovian acquiesced, happy he'd be done with this jerk in another week. In fact, he'd be done with the whole business of politics and campaigning after this. His consultancy was awash in money and the time would never better to shut down and get out.

****

"Don't make us do this," Captain Furr, skipper of the *U.S.S. Obama*, begged of Admiral Page as they cruised at five knots outside the Golden Gate, the entrance to San Francisco Bay. "I can't imagine anything more unsafe or more hair brained."

The captain and the admiral were hashing the matter out in private in Furr's day cabin, away from listening ears on the bridge.

"I can't do anything about it. I'm as furious as you are," the admiral retorted, angry with the whole insane situation. "We've got SecDEF, SecF&A, and the Deputy CNO, Admiral Hanrahan, aboard for the grand entrance through the Golden Gate. This is what they're demanding. It's supposed to be the centerpiece of the Pride Afloat Parade.

"Gay Daze on the Bay, is more like it, with aircraft carriers being their prized floaties," commented Furr bitterly.

"Watch that tone when you're out on the bridge, Captain," snapped Page.

"I'm just saying, sir, that it's hairy enough going under the Golden Gate Bridge in an aircraft carrier when there's no other shipping around you. The top of the mast barely clears the underside of the bridge, and that's only if you're near the center of the span. How are two carriers supposed to squeeze through side-by-side? There's absolutely no room for error, and we've got no experience maneuvering with the *Roosevelt*. They've got a green crew, still working up to a competent level of sea handling."

"The orders are straight from DCNO Hanrahan," responded Page.

"He's not in our chain of command, sir. Can't we appeal to CF3?" Furr asked, referring to the commander of the Third Fleet, under whose command they had fallen when they crossed the International Date Line on their way home across the Pacific.

Page thought about the potential political fallout of that course of action for one millisecond. "SecDEF wants this, too. We're outgunned on this, so let's just do it with a smile."

"I can't begin to understand the rationale behind such a dangerous and unnecessary maneuver, sir."

"Well, Captain, that's why you and I are just simple sailors. We don't appreciate the finer nuances of political symbolism. Apparently *Obama* and *Roosevelt* passing under the bridge side-by-side represent a gigantic equal sign."

"An equal sign?"

"Yeah, you know. All forms of sexuality are equal to one another."

The infuriated Furr couldn't help himself. "And SecFAGO, this Cil Borgasma, has his/her/its hands wrapped tight around the balls of SecDEF and the DCNO. How did the United States Navy ever get sucked into this kind of B.S.? Or maybe 'sucked' is a politically incorrect word nowadays."

"Like I said, Captain, watch that tone or you'll get us both cashiered."

****

Up on the highest deck, atop the *Obama's* flight bridge, two quartermasters snapped odd looking flags onto a line in preparation for running them up the mast when their ship approached the Golden Gate Bridge.

"I get this big rainbow pennant," said one, "but what do these other flags stand for? These colors are really weird and pukey."

His shipmate consulted the documentation their division chief had given them. "The one with the three way symbol is for transgender, the one with the obscene lips is called the Lipstick Lesbian Pride flag, then you've got your Leather Pride with the heart and your Bear Brotherhood with the paw print."

"Bear Brotherhood?"

"Yeah, fat, bearded guys with small dicks."

"Oh, yeah. I've seen some of that stuff on Tumblr. On my way to finding the hot babes," he quickly added.

"That one with the black and purple bars is the Gender Fluid Pride flag."

The first sailor made a face. "Gender...fluid? I don't get it but it sounds gross. What's this one with the-"

"Belay that chatter and get those flags bent on!" snarled the chief, who'd come up behind them unnoticed. "We're about to run them up."

He stepped away.

"Damned if I understand why this stuff is any business of the Navy's," he muttered to himself.

****

The two massive ships rendezvoused at the entrance to the Golden Gate under a sparkling sun, slowly converging as they approached the iconic bridge spanning the strait. The tide was running, which would complicate ship handling during the tight squeeze under the bridge.

F&A Secretary Borgasma and Defense Secretary Alioto were unaware of the turmoil and white knuckles that their request was causing on the navigation bridge, and would have been unconcerned had they realized. All the hustling and bustling going on around them is what sailors did. The Navy was there to let them show off their power to their peers.

Admiral Hanrahan stood nearby, but not too close. The rotund Borgasma wore some sort of Maoist pajama suit with a series of skirts layering the waist, and clown-like facial paint that didn't hide several days' worth of stubble. SecF&A had a bias against regular bathing and was ripe despite having applied what smelled like floral and fish scented perfumes.

The bloated Alioto, standing next to Borgasma, was oblivious to the piercing odor and munched away on food he'd brought with him from the VIP reception on the hangar deck. A steward stood to SecDEF's right holding a plate piled with hors-d'oeuvres. Alioto swiftly speared them with a kabob stick and stuffed them into his mouth, chewing nonstop like a starved dog.

As they approached the bridge, the *Roosevelt* loomed close on the port side and the VIP threesome became aware of the shouting going on between Captain what's-his-name and the helmsman.

"Excuse me a moment," said Hanrahan as he briskly strode toward the helm.

"That big, big ship is getting *so* close," cried Borgasma in a fluting voice.

Admiral Page was shouting into a radio mike for *Roosevelt* to veer away.

"Bastard's misjudged the tide!" yelled Furr over the throbbing wail of the collision alarm before an enormous jolt knocked everyone from their feet, followed by tortured metal screeching like the end of the world.

People watching from the Golden Gate Bridge saw the two supercarriers scrape against one another as they fought to get out from under the confining span, flight decks crumpling and locking together until the hulls underneath made contact. Something collided with the underside of the bridge and set up a vibration that sent people fleeing. *Obama* and *Roosevelt* were carried beyond the bridge and out into the bay on sheer momentum, fused together into a 220,000 ton mass of useless steel.

Hanrahan had regained his feet and watched the destruction unroll in disbelief, ducking as a portion of the mast came down after making contact with the Golden Gate Bridge. He heard Alioto grunting to his feet and ordering the steward back down to the hangar deck for more food. SecDEF was wearing contents of the first plate on his suit coat. Cil Borgasma sat on the deck crying, tears making streaks in the clown paint, sobbing that their entrance, their grand moment, had been ruined.

Hanrahan couldn't get away from this freak show fast enough.

A lot of naval careers aboard these two ships had just been ended, and the disastrous maneuver had been undertaken on Hanrahan's direct order. Suddenly, his secret deal with Tikriti and his collusion with General Bartz was looking very smart, the promised payoff a sanctuary from the storm about to break over Hanrahan's head.

Standing near Hanrahan, Admiral Page regarded the VIP entourage with disgust. Because of these dangerous fools, the U.S. Navy suddenly didn't have a single deployable aircraft carrier. *Obama* and *Roosevelt* would be a year in repairs, probably longer, after they figured out a way to pull the two ships apart. God help America's forces overseas if major trouble erupted there.

10

Foster Hathaway, Secretary of the Treasury, had a quarter interest in an upscale bar and grill in Georgetown, and when Lucian Wall, Chairman of the Federal Reserve, had asked for a private meeting, Hathaway suggested they meet there. They'd done it before, entering through the kitchen from the alley and taking one of the booths at the very back where they wouldn't be seen by anyone but the restaurant staff.

After a lunch of Rueben sandwiches and iced tea, they turned to business.

"Have you been watching the treasury market?" Wall asked.

Hathaway pondered that. Of course he watched the treasury market, but perhaps not the aspect of it Wall was asking about.

"Specifically, Lucian?"

"The reinvestment rate."

"Yeah. It's sagging a bit. Is that what's bothering you? You look like you're not getting much sleep."

"It's not sagging 'a bit', Foster. It's going into freefall. The Chinese rollovers we negotiated are hiding it for now, but it's accelerating. I'm getting feedback from the other central banks that buying is picking up in bonds denominated in anything other than dollars."

While that sank in, Hathaway flagged down their waiter. "Bring me a Scotch and soda. Make it a double, and easy on the soda."

He turned to Wall. "If I'd known the topic you wanted to discuss, I wouldn't have wasted time drinking iced tea. I'll admit to being distracted lately, trying to figure out some way to do something with Palma's fake yuan notes. The damned things have been showing up in bales, and I'm building a play fort in my office with them. Best idea I could come up with so far."

Wall's gloom lightened with a smile, "Jay thinks you've been laundering them, no doubt."

"Only if I had a washing machine next to my desk. I'm at my wits end. I don't dare ship the notes off to a bank to see if they can tell they're fakes. If I had any real courage I'd use them for a bonfire out in the courtyard and invite everyone down for a wiener roast."

"What will you do when Palma gets around to asking you about them?"

"Probably concoct an elaborate lie. Or maybe just tell him to go fuck himself. This whole mess he's created is wearing thin, and it just keeps getting worse."

"I've picked up some rumors that may bode ill for thee and me, Foster," Wall said quietly. "Do you know Virginia Hancock?"

"Ginnie Hancock? Sure, but I'm not certain what she does over at the Fed."

"She's a special assistant to the Board of Governors, often serving as liaison to the Treasury, which is probably how you met her. Very ambitious, and very much aware of the political ebb and flow at the Federal Reserve. Word is she's been up at the White House a lot lately, in meetings with Vance Carling and at least once or twice with the president. She hasn't mentioned this to me in any of our meetings, so she and they presumably don't want me to know about whatever they're working on."

"That's not good, Lucian. In fact," Hathaway waved his empty glass at the passing waiter, "that calls for another double. Maybe a double double. What do you think is going on?"

Wall surprised Hathaway by ordering a drink for himself, a double just like Hathaway's. He looked as serious as a bland central banker could look.

"It gets more ominous. How close a tab do you keep on Nathan Baum?"

"Not much at all. I have an undersecretary do it for me. That little butterball needs a tight leash, but that said, he's a workaholic and gets an incredible amount done as long as he's kept on the straight and narrow."

"Word has it he's been in some of the meetings with Hancock and Carling, and at least once with Palma."

"How good is that source of yours, Lucian? This isn't making my afternoon any more pleasant."

"I'd bet on its accuracy, which is why I'm telling you. I'm starting to think we've both outlived our usefulness to the president, and he's looking for replacements more amenable to his schemes."

Hathaway snorted, "Well, he won't find one in a lightweight like Baum, although you never know. Sometimes a loose cannon loves dancing with another loose cannon, but it never ends well."

They sipped their drinks in silence while grappling with the implications of what their subordinates were up to and more importantly, would they could do about it.

"What, exactly, does Baum do over at Treasury?" Wall wanted to know.

"Baum? The guy's down the totem pole a ways, reports to an assistant secretary who reports to an undersecretary who on rare occasion reports to me. An old colleague from my Wall Street days who should have informed me of Baum's comings and goings, unless she didn't know about them."

"What does the assistant secretary do, the one who's Baum's direct superior?"

Hathaway swirled his glass, his eyes narrowing as realization suddenly set in. "His boss, Ricardo Montez, runs the federal government's checkbook…all of it. Baum handles only a portion of that workload, because only a crazed workaholic could handle it all. Jesus, Lucian. Palma's found a way to screw with the books without me knowing about it!"

He pulled out his phone.

"Who're you calling, Foster?"

"Alice Tillinghast, the undersecretary Montez reports to. I've got to get to the bottom of this and find out who knows what and who's doing what."

"I wouldn't do that at this point. The ship has sailed regarding you and me, of that I am sure."

"What do you think Ginnie Hancock is up to, Lucian? I take it something very bad."

"In combination with Baum, most definitely so. She's an expert on collateralized debt, especially notes with securities or commodity assets backing them."

"Like our gold backed bond deal with the Chinese," Hathaway stated. "What else could they be looking to collateralize, though. We emptied the store right down to the dust and the cobwebs to get the Chinese deal done. In fact, that's about all that's left in Fort Knox now, dust and cobwebs."

"And in the vaults of the New York Fed, too," Wall pointed out.

"Are you having any trouble over that from the 60 countries whose gold was borrowed without asking, and handed to the Chinese?"

"As a matter of fact, the Germans and the Belgians are pressing for an audit. We've stalled them for now with the 'heightened security threat' ruse and denied access. That dam won't hold much longer."

"So, what exactly…" Hathaway pondered, "…could our two nefarious underlings be up to?"

"I just don't know," Wall responded. "I wanted to give you a heads up, and I wanted to say that this journey we've made together these past four years has been a most fantastic one. I couldn't have asked for a better colleague, a genuine peer. We did the best we could with what we had to work with, and no one could have done more, but…"

"This sounds like a farewell or something, Lucian. You're alarming me."

"I think we're done, Foster."

"Done? Surely not done. How can Palma manage without you and me? Definitely not with third and fourth stringers like Hancock and Baum. They'd sink the ship in no time."

"I don't just mean us. I mean everyone, everywhere. I mean that we've gone beyond the tipping point and we just haven't realized it yet."

"Certainly I've felt that way at times, Lucian."

"It's more than a feeling. It's the math. We've rolled up 70 trillion dollars in debt and the bill is coming due. Our creditors are finally realizing we can't pay the interest anymore, let alone the principal, and they're bailing out instead of rolling over. We're out of cash and have no way of getting more without doing something terrible and self-destructive to get it. It's no longer something abstract and out on the horizon. The tipping point is here. For the sake of our association, whatever its ultimate fruits, whatever its impact on the world, I wanted to say thank you and goodbye."

Hathaway stared at him, twirling the ice cubes in his empty tumbler. "Are you resigning?"

"There's no point. Palma isn't going to let us get away. I'll pretend to continue running the Fed, but I'm actually going to be taking time out to enjoy my last bit of freedom before he drops the hammer, which will be soon. Think about it, Foster. The shit's about to hit the fan and Palma will need sacrifices to toss to the howling mob."

"That's a grim way to visualize things, but I can't deny the validity of your conclusion. We can't run away from Palma, and the ax *will* fall on us first. I should have been more awake to all of this. I'll have to have my tailor measure me for special shirt cuffs, one's that will fit stylishly over the other kind of cuffs."

"I'm going to trust you with a very important piece of knowledge, Foster, and that is that Palma will not get away with what he's done to this country, or with what he's intending to do to us."

"I don't know about that, Lucian. We're the perfect scapegoats, and to a large degree deservedly. Palma never signed anything, never allowed any record to be created that might incriminate him. We're screwed in that regard. We'll look like the rogues in the matter, and he'll deny knowing anything about it."

"I have recordings of our meetings with him on Air Force One."

"That's not possible. Palma had everything swept ten times over. No bug would have gone undetected."

"Do you remember my silver cufflinks? My lapel pin? They contain nanotechnology that allows them to appear as solid metal to detection devices sweeping for bugs, but they record very clearly and store data at a molecular level. I have a close friend, an MIT grad, who developed the technology. No one has it but him. The government doesn't know it exists."

"What will you do with it?" Hathaway's head was spinning at the earth shattering ramifications, but not spinning too hard to prevent him from waving for another drink.

"I've given the recordings to a trusted party who, at the appropriate time, will release them to the media and the Internet, along with voice pattern data proving their authenticity. I won't release them now with things as fragile as they are economically. I don't want to be the catalyst that triggers the downfall of our world, but when it comes, as soon it will, the main culprit will not escape the consequences of his deeds."

Hathaway sat, overwhelmed and mechanically sipping his drink. Finally he said, "Lucian, you really know how to enliven a lunch."

****

Election Day, November 8th, 2028, was the most corrupt ever witnessed in the 252 year history United States of America, but few knew the scope of it since the media was part and parcel of it, bought with a river of funds directed their way by Paul Jovian's campaign machine.

The media's competition in the business of reporting of the truth, the wild and woolly Internet, was down all day throughout most of the country.

The media itself had developed a case of selective blindness.

It was blind to the wholesale busing of hordes of new arrivals from south of the border to polling places, the free food set out for them, and the cash and debit cards openly handed to them by Jovian's campaign operatives after they had voted.

It was blind to the fact that volunteers who normally manned the polling places had been detained by the police while Jovian's operatives took their places by the voting machines.

It was blind to thugs that gathered in districts hostile to President Palma and kept voters from entering the voting booths there.

It was blind to the loss of the records of votes not favoring Palma and the miraculous finding of other votes that did, provenance not known.

It was blind and stone deaf and would remain so for a long time after Election Day had ended, though at dusk its sight was keen enough to make an early call in favor of Jay Palma, who was serendipitously prepared at that unexpectedly early hour to take his victory lap at a hotel ballroom in downtown DC., with Vice President Al Morse waving at his side.

Even the media couldn't remain blind to what happened next.

****

Vance Carling had all but gotten down on his knees, begging Palma not to put the husk of Al Morse up on stage for the victorious occasion. Far too much could go wrong, but Palma wouldn't listen.

Two weeks prior, Morse's doctors had been sent packing, pledged to silence on pain of death. Frank Izzo, an army corpsman busted for distributing drugs on base when he was stationed in Korea, had taken over Morse's daily care with the promise that if things went smoothly, Izzo could stay out of Fort Leavenworth. Assisting him was a huge slab of meat named Dort Kruller, an ex-navy bosun's mate whose muscles were as massive as his brain was small.

They'd carefully extracted Morse from his sarcophagus and staged him in a wheelchair after fitting him with the motorized exoskeleton Carling had provided to them. The thing was confusing to operate but Carling ordered them to figure it out. The fewer people who saw Morse, the better, Carling insisted. Morse wasn't due on stage for three hours, so Izzo and Kruller had ample time to get it sorted.

"Do not, under any circumstances, screw this up," Carling warned them as he was leaving, "or you'll spend the rest of your lives in Leavenworth."

It was very frustrating. They could get Morse to raise his arm, but for some reason he would wave only half of the time, and the other half of the time his hand would freeze in place with a backward tilt, like Hitler receiving a salute. There seemed to be a pattern to the sequence, so Izzo paused the exoskeleton at the point where he thought Morse's next iteration would be the waving and not the saluting.

The clock had gotten away from them and when Carling checked in he found them far from ready.

"Get his make up on and get him dressed. You're running out of time, Izzo."

"Yes sir, Mr. Carling! We're getting it done. We'll be all set in thirty minutes."

"You'd better be, Izzo, because that's cutting it close."

After Carling left, Izzo got out the cosmology supplies, donned latex gloves, and started working on Morse's face. It took a lot of cream to hide the dead, blue pallor and a long time to rub it in.

"I ain't no make-up artist," he complained to Kruller. "They used to have a whole crew of people working on this guy before his appearances, according to the doc I took over from. How do they expect us to do everything? Robotics, make-up, getting him dressed with all the hoses and wires running into his back. What are we, wizards?"

Kruller grunted something about the time.

"Shit! We gotta get everything copacetic here. Look around for something I can wrap around his lower face, and some gloves to cover these claws."

Izzo had only managed to cover Morse's forehead and ears with the make-up. He abandoned that effort and looked for Morse's wig and hat, then started getting him dressed. The best Kruller could find in the way of a muffler was a pillow case from the sarcophagus. It was yellowed, but would have to do.

"Help me with his arms," Izzo ordered the big man. They wrestled a suit coat onto Morse that had been split most of the way down the back, mortician style. The hoses and wires were bundled out of sight behind Morse's body, running to a wheeled cart containing batteries, pumps, and reservoirs of necessary fluids. They attached the cart to back of the wheelchair.

The final touches involved fitting on Morse's gloves, wig, hat, and sunglasses, and wrapping the pillowcase around his neck and lower face like a scarf in order to hide his gaping mouth, which Kruller had found disturbing because it made him think of the mask in the *Scream* movies, or the victims of the well woman in *Ring*.

Carling dropped in, out of breath. He had come up from below the stage where he'd stationed a reluctant Secret Service agent near the main power breaker for the entire ballroom complex. His sense of foreboding had grown all afternoon, and he couldn't stop himself from setting up a plan B. He was in direct radio contact with the agent at the switch, having told the man to act without hesitation if Carling ordered him to kill the juice.

"What is all this?" he demanded when he saw what they'd done with Morse.

"It's the best we could do, Mr. Carling," Izzo answered defensively. "He looks like a guy battling a bad cold, if you don't look too closely."

"You should have asked me first before wrapping him up like this. Well, we're out of time now. The president is taking his bow in five minutes. Let's roll the V.P. to the elevator and get him up there."

The stage was cloaked behind closed curtains, the cheering crowd on the other side making the noise they'd been hired to. Palma was getting a last pass from his make-up people. He looked askance at the bundled up form of Morse.

They got Morse into position just in time, situated between Palma and the wing of the stage where Izzo and Kruller would be, working the controller that would cause Morse's arm to wave. Carling stood next to them.

With fanfare in the form of the swelling theme to *Rocky*, the curtains both swung smoothly aside, unlike the disaster in Los Angeles two months ago, at the grand conclusion of the convention. The ballroom was large enough to accommodate 20,000 people, and a Jumbotron hanging from the ceiling showed close up images of the victorious president and his running mate in high def.

"Make him start waving," Carling hissed at Izzo, who keyed the controller for the exoskeleton. Nothing happened.

"What the fuck?" Izzo muttered, keying the device again. The applause was beginning to die down in expectation that Palma and Morse would speak. Morse looked odd and inert next to the energized president.

Kruller lurched in panic and rushed across the stage intent on getting Morse's arm up.

"Get back here!" Carling shouted before being pushed aside by a Secret Service agent racing to intercept Kruller, who looked more like an attacker than an aide, triggering the agent's attack dog instincts. Just before Kruller reached Morse, the agent made a flying tackle, their bodies slamming into the side of the wheelchair. Morse's hat, wig, sunglasses, and scarf all went flying.

People seeing the image on the Jumbotron or on their TVs at home couldn't understand what they were looking at. Instead of a grinning, waving Al Morse, they beheld a gaping corpse with dead, blue skin atop its barren skull, and eyes rolled back to show only the whites, which were actually a bright, Sulfurous orange-yellow. All in high def.

Everyone on stage stood stock still and silent, too shocked to move or speak. The only exception was Carling, speaking urgently into his walkie talkie.

A woman on the ballroom floor broke the silence with a piercing scream before everything went dark.

To be continued…